THE CASE OF THE SLINGSHOT SNIPER

By the Same Author

The Case of the Slingshot Sniper

A McGURK MYSTERY

BY E. W. HILDICK
ILLUSTRATED BY LISL WEIL

MACMILLAN PUBLISHING COMPANY
New York

Copyright © 1983 E. W. Hildick
Illustrations copyright © 1983 Macmillan Publishing Company
All rights reserved. No part of this book may be reproduced
or transmitted in any form or by any means, electronic or
mechanical, including photocopying, recording or by any
information storage and retrieval system, without
permission in writing from the Publisher.

Macmillan Publishing Company,
866 Third Avenue, New York, N.Y. 10022
Collier Macmillan Canada, Inc.
Printed in the United States of America

10 9 8 7 6 5 4 3 2 1

Library of Congress Cataloging in Publication Data
Hildick, E. W. (Edmund Wallace), date.
The case of the slingshot sniper.
(A McGurk mystery)
Summary: The McGurk Detective Organization
comes up against a clairvoyant rival while attempting
to solve a case of vandalism.
[1. Mystery and detective stories] I. Weil, Lisl, ill.
II. Title. III. Series.
PZ7.H5463Cavc 1983   [Fic]   82–20913
ISBN 0–02–743920–8

CONTENTS

The Four Flying Fingers Strike Again

CRASH! BAM! WHIZZ! CLATTER!

The special meeting of the McGurk Organization sure started off with a bang *that* morning!

And if those words look familiar, you're right. They're the words I started with in The Case of the Four Flying Fingers.

But don't worry. I, Joey Rockaway, the Organization's record-keeper, am not getting lazy. I have used the exact same words because the exact same thing *did* happen.

Except that the first time it was in spring and now it was fall—the Saturday of the Columbus Day weekend.

Everything else was the same, though. Like with the first time, *this* special meeting was to decide what to do over the holiday period. . . .

Wanda Grieg had been all for taking it easy.

"The weather's beautiful, McGurk. I say we spend the weekend outdoors."

"Doing what?" said McGurk. "Climbing trees? I see you're dressed for it."

Wanda was wearing her oldest jeans, frayed and faded, with the stitched-on flower pattern. Her long blond hair was swept back, ready for action.

She shrugged.

"Why not? We don't have a case. Besides, we've only just finished the last one."

She glanced at the battered violin case hanging from a hook on the wall in the place of honor. Right next to the handcuffs Patrolman Cassidy had given us.

We all glanced at it. The Case of the Felon's Fiddle had been one of our toughest. We had tracked down a stash of very valuable stolen diamonds and there had been a long article about it in last weekend's newspaper. With pictures of us taken in this very basement, the Headquarters of the McGurk Organization.

McGurk's expression softened. The green eyes began to glow out of the bunch of freckles. His red hair seemed to light up.

I guess we were all feeling very proud. The only difference was in the way it affected us. Four of us felt we'd earned a breather. Satisfied with a job well done.

Our science expert, Brains Bellingham, blinked wisely behind his big round glasses.

"I think Wanda is right, McGurk. We could use the break. Not just to waste time, though. We could brush up on some of our skills."

"Like what?"

"Like going out and collecting soil samples. A good crime laboratory always has a collection of soil samples. Like if they find dirt under a dead man's fingernails, they can check on where he was just before he got murdered."

"Good thinking, Officer Bellingham. If we can't find a real case, that sounds like a useful thing to do."

"So long as it's outdoors," said Wanda, gazing at the sunlight that came shafting down through the basement window.

It was lighting up the dust particles over our

files: the cardboard cartons labeled MYSTERIES SOLVED and so on.

"Yeah!" said Willie Sandowsky. He stroked his long thin nose. "I could use the fresh air. My nose has been feeling kinda stuffed up lately. And it can't smell so good when it gets stuffed up."

McGurk looked worried then. He has great faith in Willie's sensitive nose, as one of the Organization's most valuable detecting instruments.

It seemed to be helping to make up his mind.

So then I chipped in.

"They're right, McGurk. Even detectives need to take time off."

Well, even as I spoke, I could see I was saying the wrong thing.

"That's just *it*, Officer Rockaway!" McGurk gave the table a slap. "Detectives *never* take time off. Not when crime's a twenty-four-hour a day, seven-day a week business."

He glared around.

"No, men. We've got to find another case. Another—"

And that's when the crash came. Exactly the same kind as that other time. An *almighty* crash.

And then we did exactly what we'd done before.

We ran out of the basement, up the steps into the yard.

Willie was in the lead. And once again he nearly fell over the garbage can, which was lying on its side.

But that's where the sameness ended.

The first time, McGurk, Brains and I had run through the scattered empty jars and cans. *This* time there was no scattered garbage. The plastic bag had not burst and it was still stuck in the can.

That time, Wanda had gone to pick up the lid. *This* time it was already being picked up by one of the perpetrators.

Which brings me to the biggest difference.

It was the same four kids, all right. But this time they weren't running. Instead, they just stood there, sort of quiet and tense-looking, grinning slightly. The way little seven- and eight-year-olds often do when somebody catches them doing something they shouldn't.

"Hi!" said the leader.

He was wearing a regular red baseball cap instead of the feather stuck in a red sweatband that he'd worn before. But I'd have recognized him anyway. He had the kind of look McGurk himself has.

It made no difference that his hair was brown, or that he had smudges of dirt instead of freckles, or that his eyes were blue.

It was the look in those eyes that was the same. Steady. Serious. Fierce.

Leader's eyes.

"Hi nothing!" growled McGurk. "What kind of game do you think you're playing?"

"We knocked the can over for old time's sake!" said the leader. "*That's* what we were playing! Only it wasn't playing," he added, gloomily.

"It was so you'd remember us," said the kid with the can lid.

He had big front teeth, which he kept licking nervously. I remembered they called him Jackie.

"Kind of like our calling card," said a third kid, who wore glasses.

"Yeah!" grunted the fourth, a bit dopily.

"Hi, Sam!" I said, suddenly recalling the leader's name.

"There y'are, Sam!" said Jackie. "What did I tell you? They *do* remember!"

"Who could ever forget?" said Wanda.

"Right!" said Brains. "Who could forget four little kids dumb enough to let a lady burglar use them?"

"Yeah!" said Willie. "Knocking over garbage cans. So she could see which houses still had the mess in the driveway the next day. So she could tell who was away on vacation."

"Using you dummies as fingers!" jeered McGurk.

"Are ya through with the history lesson?" snapped Sam. "I mean do you *really* want to yack about the olden days? Or do you want to talk business?"

McGurk blinked.

"Business? What business?"

"*That* business!" said Sam, stabbing a grimy finger at the notice on the basement door, the one that gave a list of some of the things the McGurk Organization did. "'Private Invester—Investich—Inves—'"

"'Private Investigations'," said Jackie, helping him out. "'Mysteries Solved, Persons Protected, Missing Persons—'"

"Yeah, yeah, yeah!" said Sam. "All that junk. Which adds up to you think you're a bunch of real smart detectives. Right, McGurk?"

McGurk drew himself up.

"We don't *think* we are, sonny! We *know* we are. So—"

"So let's see you prove it." Sam flicked his fingers. "Jackie—the bag."

Jackie was looking very serious now. Serious,

solemn and glum. They all were, as Jackie pulled out a small but bulging plastic bag and handed it to Sam.

"What's that?" said McGurk.

"Fee," said Sam, giving it a shake.

Then I realized it was full of coins.

"*Pennies?*" said Willie, sniffing disdainfully.

The kid with glasses looked mad.

"No, dummy! Those are *nickels*, mostly. Plus a few dimes."

"Our savings!" said the dopey kid, looking ready to burst into tears.

"Three dollars and fifteen cents," said Jackie, sadly. "The most we could raise."

"But it's yours if you can get us out of the jam we're in," said the glasses kid.

"Which was a frame-up," said Sam. "A dirty frame-up!"

"Wow!" murmured Wanda.

Her eyes were glistening. She looked touched. Even Brains had taken off his glasses to give them a polish, like they'd suddenly started to steam up.

As for Willie, instead of giving another disdainful sniff, he grinned awkwardly, said, "Aw, gee!"— and then let the air out through his nose in a soft gentle stream.

Only McGurk showed no sign of weakening. His eyes got narrow and even harder. Like chips of sharp green glass.

"We'll talk about fees later. *If* we decide to take the case. So what's the trouble? *What* jam?"

2 An Evil Influence?

Now McGurk wasn't being mean. It's just the way he gets whenever a possible case is mentioned. Alert. Keen. Eager to get all the details.

These details were sure hard to get. They came out in such a rush.

"They say we've been throwing rocks!"

"Breaking windows!"

"At this old lady's house."

"Only we *weren't!*"

"All we were doing was picking up pine cones in her yard."

"*Pine cones?*"

That question came from Wanda, our tree expert,

in such a loud surprised tone it made the kids stop.

"Huh?"

"You said you were collecting *pine cones? You?* What for?"

"What does *that* matter?" said Sam.

"Answer the officer!" snapped McGurk, with his eyes in even narrower slits. "Why pine cones?"

"Because there was pine cones in the old lady's yard."

"Nowhere near the house. We weren't bothering nobody. Just picking up—"

"*Why?*" roared McGurk. "*Why* were you collecting pine cones?"

Sam glared back. Then he turned to Jackie, sighed, and said:

"You tell him."

"For kindling," said Jackie, wearily.

"To sell for kindling," said the glasses kid. "Some folks like to light their fires with them."

"It's a great way of making money," said Jackie.

"And what's wrong with making money?" said the glasses kid, eying the bag of coins. "Huh?"

"Anyway," said Sam, "they said we'd been doing the breaking."

"Just because we were *there!*"

"Picking up pine cones. Not rocks. And who ever broke a window with a pine cone?"

"Besides," said Jackie, "it would have been dumb blaming *us* for the windows."

"Oh?" said McGurk. "And why?"

"Because it's been going on for years," said Sam. "We weren't big enough to throw rocks when it first started. Years ago. Years and years."

"Well," said Jackie, "just *over* a year, anyway."

"Like I said!" growled Sam.

"And if you don't believe us," said Jackie, digging into a pocket, "it says so in the paper."

He pulled out a crumpled, raggedly torn newspaper clipping.

"The *Gazette*," said Sam, as McGurk took the clipping. "A few days ago."

Here is a copy of it:

VANDALS AT WORK AGAIN ON PILSEN HOME?

For over a year, the back windows of the Pilsen residence have been a target for vandals. Hardly a month goes by without another attack. The latest came two days ago.

"Tried everything"

"We've tried everything," said Miss Elspeth Pilsen, niece of the owner, Mrs. Violetta Pilsen. "Chicken wire. We hired guard dogs. Other methods. And, sure —for a time they work. But as soon as we take the wire down or call the dogs off it happens again."

More baffling

Making the problem more baffling is the layout of the property: a rambling old Victorian house, one of the last of its kind in the Park Avenue North area. Tall hedges and trees surround the house.

"To get a shot at the windows, they'd have to get inside that ring of trees," says Miss Pilsen. "And just today I caught some kids in there. They weren't actually throwing rocks. But that's how vandals do get started, being where they've no business to be."

Police theory

The police department's theory is that no single person is responsible. "Once a house gets known as a target," a spokesman said, "other vandals come along to try their hand."

Mrs. Pilsen disagrees. "This is systematic. I believe an Evil Influence is at work."

She refused to go into details, however.

McGurk looked up. He gave Sam a nod. He was *very* interested in the case now. Then he gave me a scowl.

"This is the first time I heard about this. How come you didn't tell me about the newspaper report?"

He spread the scowl around the rest of us—like only *we* ever get to see the newspapers. Like he was always too busy or something.

I shrugged.

"I remember reading about it one of the earlier times. But since it didn't seem all that urgent, I didn't bother."

McGurk glowered.

"Huh! If you *had* told me, it wouldn't have gone on all this time. *That's* for sure. . . ." Now it was Sam's turn to get a piece of the scowl. "I suppose the kids here in this report were you guys?"

"Right! So—"

"So what are you worried about? It says they have no real evidence."

"Sure! But that doesn't stop 'em from *suspecting* us."

"And they suspect us, all right!" said Jackie.

"And we don't like cops suspecting us," said the glasses kid.

"Suspecting us," explained Jackie, "means the next time windows get smashed at that stupid old house, the cops'll be coming straight to *our* houses."

He spoke like he knew all this from experience.

"Yeah!" said Sam. "And then our folks'll get really tough with us."

"Splitting us up, saying we're a bad influence on each other!"

A murmur of sympathy went up. Even McGurk seemed convinced now. Their story sounded so genuine.

"All right," he said. "I believe you. We'll take the case."

"Terrific!" said Jackie.

"Only remember this," said McGurk, stern again. "The cops *don't* believe you. So leave it all to us. Don't go near the place until we've solved the mystery. Because if there's another attack on the Pilsen house and you're seen anywhere around, the cops'll only be more certain that you're the perpetrators. Got it?"

"O.K.," said Sam. "That makes sense. Only we'd like a receipt."

"Receipt?"

"Yeah." Sam shook the bag. "For the fee. Because

if you *don't* clear our names, we'll want our money back."

McGurk waved the bag aside. He was getting impatient. Also the Organization treasury was pretty flush at the time. The *Gazette* had paid us seventy-five dollars for our exclusive story about the diamonds. And with that kind of money in the old tin box under McGurk's bed, he could afford to be a bit picky about the kids' nickels and dimes.

"Later," he said. "You can give it to us when we've busted the case. Which won't be for *another* year if you don't beat it and let us get started."

That was enough for the kids.

As soon as they'd gone, Wanda sighed and said:

"It's all very well saying 'Let us get started,' McGurk. But *where?*"

She'd been looking at the clipping. I guess she'd been wondering what we'd let ourselves in for. I mean this was a case that had been baffling everyone—police included—for over a year. With possibly dozens of different perpetrators. Not to mention the old lady's theory about spooks!

"Yes," I said. "Where *do* we start?"

"Where?" said McGurk. "At the scene of the crime, of course! Where else?"

3 The Scene of the Crime

Although Park Avenue North is long, we soon found the Pilsen place. Like it said in the newspaper, there were very few of the original houses left. Most had been replaced by high-rise apartment buildings or groups of ranch-type houses. And there were signs posted that said where others were in the process of being replaced.

Something else made our search easier, too. Most of the remaining old houses looked very uncared for, with peeling paintwork, overgrown grass and front lawns littered with junk. Among all this, the Pilsen house stood out as something special.

It may have been dwarfed by the high-rise building opposite, but it still looked well kept. It was the only house with a tall hedge, and that hedge looked thick and healthy and carefully trimmed. Even the trees that rose above it, just inside the hedge, seemed specially groomed, firs and pines and cedars, their pointed tops all in a line.

And the fancy spires and turrets of the house, visible between the treetops as we approached from the side, looked in good condition. The white paint-work sparkled and the dark green trim glowed.

"Yes," I said, pointing to the neat black and white sign at the end of the driveway. "I *knew* this would be the one."

The sign read:

V. PILSEN

NO TRESPASSING

McGurk was looking thoughtful. He nodded toward the front of the house, most of which could be seen from the driveway entrance.

"Anyone could throw rocks at the windows from *here*," he said. "But all the damage has been done in back, according to the newspaper. And if there's no gap in the hedge there, the lady's right. It means the perpetrators just had to be inside the yard."

"Well, it should be easy to check," said Brains.

"There's nothing to stop us from crossing the land on either side."

He was right. The houses next to the Pilsen place had been pulled down. The rubble had been cleared away and the ground leveled, leaving the grass and weeds to grow thick—with a few tromped-down crisscrossed paths.

"There's been plenty of traffic here," said McGurk, leading the way.

The land at the back had also been leveled. But here, besides patches of long grass, there was still a lot of rubble: piles of timber and bricks; tangles of rusty pipes; and broken glass everywhere.

"No shortage of ammunition," said McGurk, kicking a hunk of brick before turning to inspect the Pilsens' back hedge.

There was no gap here. Not of the regular type anyway, like the driveway entrance. There were a few small irregular holes, just like in any hedge. But these looked hardly big enough for dogs or cats, let alone kids.

No, if anything, it was thicker than the hedge at the front. Even the line of trees inside the hedge looked closer together, making a kind of two-story hedge of their own.

"O.K.," said McGurk. "Now we'll go talk to the lady."

The first thing that struck me as we entered the driveway was the neatness of the grass, rich and green even this late in the year, and beautifully smooth and short. On both sides of the driveway, the lawns swept down to the trees, where the grass just seemed to be shaved off into the brown carpet of pine and fir needles.

"One thing's for sure," said McGurk. "Whoever broke the windows would have to bring rocks in with them. They couldn't count on picking up any in here."

"Right!" said Brains. "Even the gravel we're walking on seems to be specially graded. Nothing bigger than a pea."

The doorbell at the front was made of brass, shiny and clean. When McGurk rang, the door opened at once, like the woman had been watching us approach.

"Yes?" she said, giving us all a quick, sweeping, suspicious look.

"Mrs. Pilsen?" said McGurk.

"No. I'm *Miss* Pilsen." The woman looked slightly annoyed. "What do you want?"

I could understand McGurk's mistake. Her dark hair was streaked with gray. Also the way she dressed made her look older: in dull colors—like the browny-fawn sweater and thick black skirt—with heavy lace-up brown shoes. There were bits of fluff all over the sweater and the skirt zipper had broken and been fixed with a big safety pin.

But her face was young: plump and smooth, with a loose mouth that kept smiling on and off. It was one of those smiles that turn down at one corner, a twisted smile.

"I'm Jack P. McGurk, ma'am. Head of the Mc-Gurk Organization. Detectives. These are my officers. Here's my ID."

"Is this some kind of joke?"

"No, ma'am. No way. We're making a serious investigation. On behalf—"

"Did anyone here ask you to? I know *I* didn't."

Her eyes were flitting from face to face, like she was still not sure whether this wasn't a joke.

"No, ma'am. Our clients are the four kids who got accused of breaking your windows. Sam—"

"Oh, *them!* Well, nobody actually accused them right out. But they *were* behaving suspiciously. And they *were* trespassing. And—" She broke off. "But what am I doing, talking about it to *you?*" she went on. "You're only children yourselves. What do *you* know about—"

"Investigations, ma'am?" Now McGurk was looking annoyed. "I told you. We're the McGurk Organization. We've worked on all kinds of mysteries. Only a couple of weeks ago we helped trace some stolen diamonds. It was in the papers. Here—read this if you don't believe me!"

Then he pulled out *our* clipping, much bigger than the one Jackie had been toting around.

"But—"

"*You heard what the boy said, Elspeth! Even I read about that!*"

Miss Pilsen nearly jumped out of her baggy old skirt at the sound of the dry crackling voice. It even caused a bit of a tremor to run through some of us, too. It had seemed to come from nowhere, like a ghost voice.

Then a second woman stepped out of the shadows behind the first.

"I'm *Mrs.* Pilsen," she said. "The owner of the property."

She *was* old. She was very thin, very frail, very wrinkled. The top of her head reached only just above her niece's shoulders. But she held herself very erect, and the eyes that looked out of the network of wrinkles were clear and gray, steady and sharp. *Her* mouth wasn't loose. It was tight, thin, firm. And *her* clothes weren't sloppy. True, the color was dull—a kind of metallic gray. But there wasn't a speck of dust or a fold out of place on that plain shirt or those crisp pants.

"Yes, ma'am. How are you? And we're—"

"As to how I am, young man, the answer is worried. And as to who you are, I heard what you were saying." She turned to the younger woman. "You should learn to seize a good opportunity when it arises, Elspeth. If these children are smart enough to find missing diamonds, they might very well be useful here."

"But—"

"But nothing, Elspeth. Really! You're the one who's always saying that kids have been doing the damage. Very well. Then maybe it will take a bunch of kids to track them down. *You've* never been able to."

"No, Aunt. But—"

"So let them investigate. I never did believe it was those little boys, anyway. You were far too hasty over that. *However. . . .*"

Here the old lady paused and gave us a slow thoughtful look. It wasn't hard or searching. In fact it was more of a worried look, as if she was seeing something far-off—something in a murky haze.

". . . I myself think it's something more. Something worse than any kids. Something . . . *evil!*"

The warm sun was on our backs. But I for one felt a little shiver go through me.

"Anyway," she said, brisk again, "give them whatever help they need in their investigation, Elspeth. Where would you like to begin, young man?"

"Uh—around the back, ma'am," said McGurk.

"Very well. Take them there, Elspeth."

The younger woman's smile wobbled off and on.

"Yes, Aunt." Then, to us, "Come with me, please."

"It looks like we've gotten ourselves another client now, McGurk," whispered Wanda, as we followed Miss Pilsen.

McGurk nodded.

"A sensible old lady," he murmured.

I guessed this was partly because Mrs. Pilsen had shown the Organization *some* respect. But that didn't account for McGurk's frown.

"Sure!" I said. "So—?"

"So we can't just laugh it off," he said, keeping his voice low.

"Laugh what off?"

"That stuff about an Evil Influence," said McGurk, darkly.

4 The Box of Rocks

As soon as we'd turned the corner and were in the back yard, Miss Pilsen said:

"You must excuse my aunt. She really is one very worried old lady."

She herself looked more relaxed now.

"You mean about the broken windows?" said Mc-Gurk, gazing up at the back of the house.

"Yes. It's been going on so long, you see. She's very stubborn, but it's beginning to get her down."

"I can imagine," said Wanda.

Miss Pilsen's twisted smile twitched on and off.

"I keep suggesting that we move away from here," she said. "The neighborhood's ruined anyway—all this new building. But she won't listen. She's lived in this house for more than fifty years and she says she intends to die here."

Willie grunted.

"Yeah. My grandma's like that. She—"

"The more worried she gets, the more stubborn she gets," said Miss Pilsen, cutting in. "I'm afraid she'll crack up before long, though. Then she'll just *have* to leave."

At the words "crack up" McGurk turned. Now he said, in a brisk businesslike tone:

"Exactly which windows have been hit, ma'am?"

Miss Pilsen shrugged.

"Most of them. At one time or another over the past fourteen months. Some several times."

We stared. I mean that was a lot of broken glass. There was certainly no shortage of targets.

Here's a copy of the rough sketch I drew at the time. Where there's a number, it tells you how many times the window had been hit, as of that date. Another thing to note carefully is that the windows on the first and second floors were mainly the sort with big fixed center sections, and smaller, sliding windows at the sides of these sections. The hits on those windows had been made in the fixed sections—the most expensive to replace.

Back Porch

We got the numbers from Miss Pilsen. She said it was most unpleasant, having to go over it all again. But McGurk insisted—very politely.

In fact even *then* McGurk claimed to be getting something useful out of those figures.

"It shows there's a sort of pattern," he said.

"What pattern?" said Brains.

"Like the windows up top. They either missed them altogether or only hit them once. I guess it's because they're smaller. Not so easy to hit."

Miss Pilsen nodded.

"Yes. I suppose so. Oddly enough, though, they were the first."

McGurk frowned. He didn't know what to say to *that*.

But Wanda had an objection to his original theory.

"How come the big one on the first floor's only been hit once?"

McGurk's frown deepened. He hates to have any of his theories shot down so quickly. Then he gave Miss Pilsen a keen look.

"Are you *sure* that's only been hit once, ma'am?"

"Positive! In fact, it hadn't been broken at all until a few days ago."

"Yes, well, I think I see the answer to that, Mc-Gurk."

Brains was blinking slowly at the window.

"Yeah? What, Officer Bellingham? Why?"

"Because as a target it's partly screened at the top by the porch roof. And at the bottom there are the rails. Kind of narrows the target area down."

"Good thinking! But how about the chicken wire, ma'am? Doesn't that keep the rocks from doing any damage?"

(I haven't shown this on the sketch, to keep the main details clear. But every window had a special screen. Instead of the usual fine mesh, this was heavy-duty crisscrossed wire.)

Miss Pilsen sighed.

"Oh, yes! It keeps the rocks out. When it's up. But you can't have your windows wired up *all* the time. So every so often, after there's been a lull for a few weeks, we take it down. You know—hoping whoever's been doing this will have grown tired of waiting."

"And they don't?" said Wanda.

"No. For instance, I took the chicken wire down on Monday. But that very evening, the dining room window was smashed." Miss Pilsen nodded toward the one behind the back porch. "It's been fixed. But you should have seen the mess. Luckily we were having our meal in the TV room, at the front."

"*Oh?*"

McGurk's question flew out like a missile itself.

"Yes. We were lucky. Someone could have gotten hurt. Badly. There was glass all over the table."

"*Has* anyone been hurt yet, Miss Pilsen?" asked Wanda.

"No." The woman looked grim. "Not yet. But it's only a matter of time, as I keep telling Aunt Violetta."

"It must have been a pretty big rock," said Brains.

"Oh, it was! They always are." She hesitated, then said, "Wait here. I'll show you."

We'd hardly had time to take another careful look at the windows before she returned.

"Wow!" gasped Willie.

He was gaping at the shoe box Miss Pilsen was carrying. It contained quite a collection of rocks.

"Are all these—?" McGurk began.

"Yes. Each one was used to smash a window. Each one was picked out of the broken glass. There are only about ten here, because I didn't start saving them right away. Then I thought the police might find them useful."

"And did they?"

She shook her head.

"They scarcely glanced at them. Said that it was next to impossible to take fingerprints off rocks like these."

Well, the police had a point there. I mean the rocks were big enough to have carried prints. Some were as big as tennis balls.

But they weren't smooth enough. Some were simply rough hunks of broken brick or concrete. And those that *were* the kind you find in the ground, lying there naturally, were all corners and ridges. Several sparkled dimly.

Brains picked out one of these.

"Maybe they wouldn't show any fingerprints at that," he said. "But they *could* tell something about where the vandals picked them up."

"Oh?" said McGurk.

"Sure!" said our science expert. "These, for instance. See that shiny stuff?"

"Bits of glass," said Willie. "Yeah."

"No. That's silicon. Quartz crystals. Are there any like this turning up in the yard, ma'am?"

"No," said Miss Pilsen. "I'd thought of that myself. But you'd have to dig down under the lawn to find any rocks here. And when you do come across one occasionally—like under the old pine needles— they're the dull sandy kind."

"There are plenty of rocks like these shiny ones in Willow Park," said Wanda. "Up on the hill, among the trees."

"Yeah!" McGurk's eyes were green slits as he gazed into the box. "And there isn't a sandy one in this bunch."

"So?" I said.

"So we've already found something out about the perpetrators."

"Have we?" said Miss Pilsen.

"Yes, ma'am. Like it makes it even more certain that our clients didn't do it. They're the kind of kids who do things on the spur of the moment. They don't come prepared."

"Some of the bricks and concrete could have been picked up just over the hedge," said Wanda.

"Sure!" said McGurk. "But it still shows that whoever did it, came here on *purpose* to bust the windows."

"And if they brought some of the rocks from somewhere as far away as Willow Park, it really shows they meant business," I said.

Miss Pilsen looked nervous. She licked her lips, gave her twisted smile, and said:

"Yes. I'm afraid you're right!"

"One thing's for sure, anyway," said Wanda.

"Wherever the rocks were picked up, they must have been *thrown* from inside the yard. With all that force."

"Not necessarily so," said Brains. He swung around. "How about from up there? Top of the trees? Someone climbing up and throwing from there?"

"Well, technically, that still *is* in the yard," I said.

But the others were more interested in this new angle than in precise English.

"Yeah!" said Willie. "The way snipers do. *They* climb trees!"

Wanda shaded her eyes and gave the treetops an expert scanning.

"Could be," she murmured. "But it would be tricky. I mean it's all right for snipers. They only have to squeeze a trigger. But it isn't the same, throwing rocks. You need room for that. A good firm foothold and room to swing your arm."

"How about a slingshot, then?" said Brains. "What if it was a *slingshot* sniper?"

"Well, yes," said Wanda. "That *would* make it easier. But not with rocks *this* size."

And although we didn't know it at the time, that was the first major breakthrough in our toughest case yet.

5 McGurk Runs a Test

Miss Pilsen had been looking very alarmed at this talk of snipers. I guessed she'd had a sudden vision of a troop of hit-men clambering about in the tree-tops. She shook her head.

"I doubt it! About anybody throwing the rocks from up there, I mean. I thought of *that*, too. But most times I run out when I hear the crash. And nobody ever is up there." She hesitated. "And surely they wouldn't be able to climb down that quickly?"

McGurk turned to our tree expert.

"Officer Grieg?"

"Well, it depends how high up they were." Then Wanda shook her head. "But no. The lower down they were, the more bushy branches would be in the way, spoiling their aim. They'd *have* to be near the top. And it would take a lot more than half a minute to climb down from there."

"You sure?"

"Well—"

"Let's *make* sure, huh? Officer Grieg, why don't you climb one right now? Then we'll time how long it takes to climb down in a hurry. With Officer Bellingham's watch."

"Sure!" Wanda glanced at Miss Pilsen. "With your permission, ma'am."

"Go ahead! I don't see what good it will do, but—"

"Scientific accuracy, ma'am!" said Brains, turning his wrist, ready.

Brains's watch is something else. As well as the local time, it tells you the date, the times in Hong Kong and London, the phases of the moon, and the points of the compass. Split-second timing is child's play to *that* instrument.

So when Wanda had reached the top of one of the cedars, and was through demonstrating how difficult it would be to throw something forcefully from up there without risking your neck, Brains said:

"O.K., Wanda. *Now!*"

Then he gave one of the buttons on his watch a click and Wanda began her downward scramble.

"Remember—you don't want to be caught!" McGurk urged her.

He didn't need to bother. Wanda is no slouch. In fact, by the time her feet had touched the ground she'd beaten her own estimated time.

"Twenty-five and three-tenths seconds!" Brains announced.

"So much for your 'a lot more than half a minute,' Officer Grieg!"

"I was thinking of somebody *else's* best time," said Wanda, with a toss of her hair. "Not an expert's."

McGurk grunted. Then he turned to Miss Pilsen. He tried to look polite and respectful.

"Uh—I wonder if—uh. . . . Well, ma'am, you see how easy it is to misjudge time. Even for an *expert*." He gave Wanda a glower. Then, with a horrible smirk: "I mean are you *sure*, ma'am—I mean absolutely certain—?"

"That it takes me less than twenty-five seconds to get out here? I should think so!" She gave a nervous giggle. "But why don't I go into the television room and you can time *me*?"

So once again Brains got his watch all set. Then he nodded and McGurk hollered the signal he'd arranged.

"*CRASH!*"

"Tinkle! Tinkle!" giggled Willie. "That's the bits of glass falling—"

"Quiet!" snapped McGurk.

Then:

"Ten and seven-tenths seconds!" our science expert announced, as Miss Pilsen burst through the back door, hugging her box of rocks like a quarterback heading for a touchdown.

"Well, that settles *that*!" said McGurk, sounding

a bit disappointed. "Looks like the treetop theory is out. Especially when you remember that the perpetrator still has to find his way back through the hedge."

"That's what I said," murmured Miss Pilsen. She put the box down on the ledge on top of the porch rails. "I knew it didn't take long for—is something wrong?"

Willie had lifted the lid of the box and was sniffing.

"No, ma'am. It's just—some kind of perfume—uh—lily of the valley, I think. But—"

"Yes. That's correct. I guess it comes from the drawer I store them in." She smiled. "I'm sorry. Did you think it might be a clue?"

Willie blushed.

"Well, no, ma'am. But what puzzled me was—"

"That's O.K., ma'am," said McGurk. "Officer Sandowsky's sense of smell often does come in useful. But I guess right now he's just trying to make up for cracking dumb jokes."

McGurk gave Willie another dirty look. Then he turned to Miss Pilsen.

"Anyway, ma'am, it seems certain the rocks were thrown from inside the yard. So why not try staking out the yard?"

Miss Pilsen sighed.

"Don't think we *haven't* tried it. The police have done it themselves. We've also hired security guards, with dogs. But there's never any incident when that happens. And of course it's far too expensive to keep someone on watch every evening, into the night, year round."

"Is that when it usually happens?" I asked.

"After dark? Yes."

"So doesn't *that* rule out kids, too?" Wanda asked.

"Not the kind that go around doing this sort of thing," said Miss Pilsen. "The parents just don't seem to care how long they stay out."

"How about see-in-the-dark cameras?" said Brains. "Infra-red. They could easily be attached to trip-wires and—"

"We tried that, too. The police arranged it. But nothing ever came of it."

"And why should it, if it's the work of Evil Forces?"

The dry voice once again seemed to crackle out of nowhere.

Then we looked up. Mrs. Pilsen had just stepped out onto the balcony under the middle second-story window.

Her voice became gentler as she said to McGurk:

"I've been admiring your thoroughness, young man. But I've been thinking—and I'm afraid you're wasting your time." Then she added, more crisply: "And there *is* one thing we haven't tried yet, Elspeth."

"Yes, Aunt? What?"

"You'll see! I'll be making the arrangements this afternoon. These children have given me an idea."

"Ma'am?" said McGurk.

But Mrs. Pilsen ignored him.

"So give them some milk and cookies, Elspeth, and let them be on their way. If my instincts are correct, we might not be needing their services after all."

Then she went in, leaving her niece to give us the milk and cookies.

"My aunt gets these peculiar notions from time to time, I'm afraid."

"That's O.K., ma'am," said McGurk, wiping the crumbs from his mouth. "It was very interesting to check all those details anyway. Useful training."

And if Miss Pilsen was fooled by that meek and mild reaction, we weren't.

Because when Jack P. McGurk gets his teeth into a case this juicy, he *never* lets go.

The gleam in his eyes was enough to tell us that!

INVESTIGATION AT SCENE
OF THE CRIME

Location : _Pilsen residence_

Subject : _Broken windows_

1. _Probably same person or persons._
   (Neighbors ?)

2. _Not a bunch of different_
   vandals each time attracted by
   publicity.

3. MOTIVE ? _Enemy? Somebody_
   with grudge ?

4. PERPETRATORS' TACTICS & M.O. :
   Watching every day ? Hole in hedge?

6 The Weeping Wizard

McGurk wasn't kidding about checking over what
we'd learned. He started in right away, as we headed
back home. And whenever we reached some definite
conclusion, he made us stop so I could write it down.

"There's nothing to beat making notes while the
details are fresh in your mind," he said, when Wanda
protested that we'd be late for lunch.

Anyway, by the time we'd reached our own
neighborhood (_very_ late for lunch) I'd jotted down
the notes shown above.

The reason we'd decided it had probably been done by the same person or group was the overall pattern. Like:

(a) The damage was *always* at the back.

(b) New damage was usually done soon after the security had been lifted.

Which led to the question about neighbors.

"I mean, the perpetrators *have* to live pretty close," said Brains. "To keep tabs like that on what's happening at the Pilsen place."

"Good thinking!" said McGurk. "Make a note about neighbors, Officer Rockaway."

The reasons we'd decided against the police theory about different vandals getting the idea from the newspaper were these:

(a) (To quote my own words.) "Dummies like that don't usually read newspapers anyway."

(b) (To quote McGurk.) "No. And if they *were* dummies, at least some of them would go for the easy hit. Like throwing the rocks at the *front* windows, from the driveway."

That led on to the note about the motive. None of us was sure what this could be. But if the damage hadn't been done by random vandals, it seemed likely that the rock-thrower or throwers had to have a grudge against the Pilsen ladies.

"Put it down, Officer Rockaway. It's an angle we have to check."

As for the notes on Method of Operation, the one about the perpetrators keeping watch every day arose from the earlier note about neighbors.

The note about the hole in the hedge, however, came partly from McGurk's impatience to follow up.

"I'm not saying this is definitely part of the M.O. But *whoever* throws the rocks has to be inside the yard to do it. Right?"

Nobody disagreed.

"O.K.," said McGurk. "So my guess is that they get in around the back or the sides someplace. Where it's dark and there aren't any passers-by. So there must be *some* sort of gap in that hedge, even if it isn't very noticeable."

"Well, possibly. But—"

" 'Possibly' nothing, Officer Grieg! I say there has to be. And right-after lunch, men, that's our next line of investigation."

The afternoon had taken a gloomy turn by the time we were back near the Pilsen house. The sun was lost behind heavy threatening clouds the color of bruises.

"Right, men!" said McGurk, as we approached the back, through the vacant lot. "You know what we're looking for. Any weak spot a person can use to squeeze through, into the yard."

We were about to start looking when McGurk pulled us up.

"Wait! We do this systematically. Wanda, Joey— you take this back section, with me. Willie, you search along the right side. Brains, take the left."

Well, the back looked pretty hopeless. Wanda did find a hole along the bottom, but barbed wire had been strung across from the inside.

McGurk turned to me.

"Any luck, Officer Rockaway?"

"No. I don't think—"

"Hey! Psst! McGurk!"

It was Willie. He'd stuck his head around the corner.

"What?"

"There's someone *in* there," he said, in a hoarse whisper. "Snooping around. Sort of sneaky."

"You sure?" said McGurk, trying to see for himself by plucking a bunch of twigs to one side. "It wasn't one of the ladies?"

"No. A kid. Down near this end of the yard. I was trying to squeeze through a gap. It wasn't wide enough—but it *was* wide enough to see through. And—"

"O.K. Good work, Officer Sandowsky!" McGurk whispered. "Go get Officer Bellingham before he makes a noise and alarms the suspect."

"Suspect?" I said.

McGurk's eyes were glowing.

"What else? . . . Come on, you two!" he rasped, beckoning to Willie and a startled-looking Brains.

Then Willie led the way around the side to the gap he'd discovered, about halfway along. Sure enough, it was too narrow to squeeze through. In fact it was hardly wide enough to *see* through. Especially for five pairs of eyes.

But by bunching close together—some crouching, some on tiptoe, and one (McGurk) flat on the ground with his head where the gap was widest—we saw the person Willie had spotted.

Luckily, he wasn't moving around much, because the gap gave only a very narrow view of one particular section of the yard. But he was standing in the corner, down near the trees, and all his movements were made on that spot.

I mean, it was *weird*, the way he was acting.

But first his description:

Tall and thin, about fourteen years old. He had

longish blond hair, almost white, which flipped and flopped around his face as he moved his head. His face was very pale—especially in contrast with the evergreens behind him and the clothes he wore, a black sweater and black jeans.

And his movements?

Like I said, weird.

He was turning slowly, on the spot, with his head thrown back and his eyes covered with one big white hand. He turned a complete circle of 360 degrees that way.

Then—still with the hand over his eyes—he bent his head down and did the full circle again, in the opposite direction.

Wanda's head was just below mine.

"Is—is he sick?" she whispered.

Willie's head was just above mine.

"More like he's nuts," he whispered. "He'd started doing that when I first saw him."

From deep down below, McGurk's voice came rasping up.

"Anyone know him?"

No one replied.

I was frowning. It was difficult to tell, but there was something familiar about the stranger's large

loose gaping mouth. He wasn't from our neighborhood, but I had a feeling I'd seen him around.

Wanda was obviously having the same thoughts.

"I've seen him before, I'm sure. But—"

"*Hey!*" Brains gasped. "What's he doing *now?*"

The blond kid had stopped rotating. Still with the
hand in front of his eyes, he was stooping. And—
yes!—he seemed to be picking something up.

Then, with a quick jerky movement, he straightened up, leaned back, flung back his picking-up
arm, and—

"He—he's taking aim!" said Wanda. "He's going
to throw something!"

Instantly, a kind of volcanic eruption took place
at the bottom of the gap.

It was McGurk, lurching to his feet.

"*Come on, men! Let's make the arrest!*"

McGurk's face was red. I guess it was with the effort
of keeping his voice down when all the time it
wanted to let loose a roar. Anyway, that set the tone.
We followed him as fast but as quietly as possible,
when he went barreling around to the front, through
the entrance to the driveway, and over the grass at
the side of the driveway (to deaden our footsteps).

I kept expecting to hear the crash of glass, but the

only sounds were the thudding of our feet. I was
beginning to think that the kid was either a lousy
shot or he believed in taking his time over his aim.
And when we burst onto the back lawn it looked
like the second of these was correct.

He was still standing there, one hand over his

eyes and the other way behind him, with his body leaning back, poised for a really powerful throw. He was so wound up, in fact, that he didn't even notice our arrival.

Only when our leader yelled, "Grab him!" and dove for the kid's throwing arm, and Willie made a clutch at his left arm, and Wanda got hold of a fistful of his sweater, and Brains sort of wrapped himself low down around the kid's knees, and I stepped around the whole swaying, struggling bunch—to cut off the intruder's retreat if he should manage to wriggle free—only then did he seem to wake up.

"*Hey!*" he hollered.

He began to jerk around. Brains lost his grip and sprawled on his face. Willie went spinning away as the kid's left hand went into action. Only McGurk and Wanda managed to hang on, and even they were sent swinging around as the kid turned completely.

"*Hey! Help me!*" he yelled, when he came face to face with me.

What he thought *I* was doing there, I don't know. Maybe he thought I was just a passer-by or something. One thing for sure, anyway: The guy was in shock. His face was whiter than ever, and tears were streaming down his cheeks.

"Just stay right where—"

I was going to say, "Just stay right where you are and you won't get hurt!"—when another voice cut in.

"*Leave him alone, you little fools! He's trying to help!*"

A thin, dry, crackling voice.

All at once the group in front of me stopped jerking around. Wanda let go of the sweater; Willie turned; Brains blinked around anxiously from where he was still sitting; and McGurk relaxed his grip—though without completely releasing the prisoner.

Mrs. Pilsen was stalking down toward us, looking furious, with Miss Pilsen right behind her, looking nervous.

"Did they hurt you?" the younger woman asked.

"No, ma'am," the kid said, giving McGurk a peevish scowl and finally snatching away his other arm. "But they broke the Mood. Destroyed it. Totally!"

"Mood?" I said.

"Yes." He gave me a less ferocious look. "I was just beginning to feel In Touch. In Touch with the Spirit World." He dabbed at his wet cheeks. "That's why I was weeping. I always weep when I start to feel In Touch." His scowl deepened. "Then these jerks came and shattered the Mood!"

Wanda had been staring hard.

Suddenly she gasped.

"Hey! Now I remember. You're the *Weeping Wizard*—right?"

The Psychic Snoegels

7 Poltergeists?

McGurk looked at Wanda as if she'd gone crazy. But for the first time since we'd barged in on him, the stranger smiled.

"That's right," he said to Wanda. "Merlin Snoegel. *You've* heard of me, too?"

"Sure! You entertain at children's parties, charity concerts, and like that. You have this mind-reading act. You and your parents. The Psychic—"

"The Psychic Snoegels—yes," said the kid. "But it isn't just an act." Merlin was beginning to look annoyed again. "I really am psychic."

"Psycho?" said Willie. "That means crazy, doesn't it?"

"No, Willie," I said quickly, catching the look in Merlin's eye. "Psychic means being able to see spirits, foretell the future, stuff like that."

"Which is why I thought he could help us," said Mrs. Pilsen. "A child psychic. If the Evil Forces are the spirits of spiteful children, what better than a living child to track them down."

McGurk gave Merlin an uneasy, almost shy look. "Well, I guess it does make sense."

Merlin nodded. His mouth had a scornful twist.

"*Sure* it makes sense! Psychics often help the *real* police. In murder cases and hunts for missing people. Even *you* must have heard of that!"

"Yeah!" grunted McGurk, coloring a little. "I've read about them. And—uh—do you think—uh— maybe this isn't the work of human beings?"

"Evil Forces!" said Mrs. Pilsen, fiercely. "As I said!"

Miss Pilsen looked like she was about to say something. But then she shrugged and gave a long worried sigh instead.

Merlin looked at Mrs. Pilsen cautiously.

"Well, not exactly *evil*, ma'am. Like I told you on the phone earlier. More *mischievous*, really." He drew himself up. "In fact, ma'am, it is my opinion that this is probably the work of poltergeists."

"They're a mischievous kind of ghost, Willie. They—"

But Brains interrupted.

"Baloney!" he said to Merlin. "Absolute baloney!" His face had become red with indignation. He'd even gotten red under his short bristly hair. "Even if there *were* such things, they wouldn't be powerful enough to toss rocks the size of these."

Merlin's way of showing indignation was different. *He* seemed to get even whiter.

"Well that's where you're wrong, see! There are cases on record where they've moved much bigger objects!"

"Not on *scientific* record! Not *scientifically* proved!"

"This *is* a science!"

"Baloney!"

I'd never seen Brains look so furious and tense. When Mrs. Pilsen touched him on the shoulder he nearly jumped out of his shoes.

"Little boy—will you stop arguing?" she said. "Can't you see this is affecting Merlin's very sensitive state?" She turned to the kid. "Did you really sense some invisible power?"

"Yes, Officer Bellingham," said McGurk. "Just be quiet!"

I could tell at a glance that McGurk was genuinely sold on this psychic business. And the respectful way he listened to Merlin's reply proved it. I groaned inwardly. If this went on much longer he'd be inviting the creep to join the Organization. And I for one was with Brains all the way in this matter.

"I was just beginning to *feel* presences," Merlin was saying, lowering his voice and half-closing his eyes. "Yes. *Presences*. More than one. . . . Something powerful . . . but childlike. . . . Watching me."

"*Sure!* That was *us!* The McGurk Org—"

"Cool it, Officer Bellingham! Go on, Merlin."

"Well, that's all." Now Merlin's eyes were wide open and his voice normal. "Then you dummies butted in and destroyed the Mood." He turned. "But tell me, ma'am. Did you ever hear of any children living here? Long ago—yes—very long ago . . . ." His voice had gotten drowsy again. He put his hand over his eyes. "A boy and a girl, maybe . . . . Yes . . . . A boy . . . and . . . and a girl. Who maybe met with an accident? . . . A—a fire? . . . Or—wait!—or drowned? Yes—drowned . . . . I see a pond . . . . Was there a pond here?"

We'd all gotten silent now. Even Brains. I mean, if this *was* an act, then it was a pretty good one.

Willie's mouth hung open.

McGurk's eyes were bulging.

Miss Pilsen and Wanda were both looking around uneasily.

And Mrs. Pilsen was frowning very thoughtfully. "Do you think, maybe—?"

"*Their* spirits? Yes, ma'am. Acting as . . . as poltergeists."

"But not *evil?*" said Mrs. Pilsen.

Still with his hand to his eyes, Merlin dipped his head.

"Uh—well—now that you mention it—yes . . . . I see . . . ."

There was a long, long pause. Nobody spoke. He started to sway. I began to wonder if he was going to faint. Then Wanda gave a little gasp and pointed to his face and I saw the tears starting to stream from under his hand. Then:

"I see them," he droned, in a far-off voice, "I see them in old-fashioned clothes . . . . And . . . and they're left on their own a lot . . . with servants. And —yes, yes!—it's the *servants* who are evil! A—a manservant and a woman. And *they* planted evil ideas in those little heads—the little boy's and the little girl's. Oh, yea! Verily! I see them! I see them!"

"*Baloney!*" Brains's howl made everyone start.

"That was on *TV!* Last *Halloween! The Twist of the Knife!* A *movie!*"

"Yes," I said. "I remember it, too! Only it was called *The Turn of the*—"

"Whatever!" said Brains. He turned to McGurk. "We don't have to stand here and listen to this, do we?"

Merlin's hand came away from his eyes. He blinked around, through his tears.

"Where—where am I?" he asked, in a little voice.

Miss Pilsen scowled at Brains.

"See what you've done, young man?"

Brains blinked up at her.

"I'm sorry. But if you really believe this junk—uh—this theory, ma'am, why don't you call in some real psychic research workers? Who'll investigate your case scientifically?"

"That's what *I've* been doing, dummy!" said Merlin, in not such a little voice.

"You!" snapped Brains. "You're nothing but—"

"Or better still," I said, giving Brains a soothing pat, then taking my hand back quickly when he looked like he'd bite it off, "why don't you get someone to get *rid* of the ghosts? Not just investigate them, but exorcise them. You know—an exorcist—a priest or a minister who'll—"

"We know what an exorcist is, thank you!" said Mrs. Pilsen. Her eyes brightened. "And yes—that is a good idea. I'm surprised we didn't think of this before, Elspeth. I'll talk to the Reverend Simpson."

Miss Pilsen looked fed up. She gave a big sigh, squeezed out one of her twisted smiles, and said:

"Yes, Aunt. Of course." Then she scowled at us. "Meanwhile, we don't want to see you around here any more. You were told this morning we wouldn't be needing your services, and—"

"Correction, Elspeth! I said we *might* not be needing them." She gave us a chilly smile. "But I still appreciate their thoroughness. Even though I still believe there are Evil Forces at work."

"You bet!" muttered Merlin.

But Mrs. Pilsen was looking at McGurk.

"Young man—consider your corporation or whatever you call it—consider it still retained to investigate the case in *your* way. But kindly give this other young man the chance to investigate *his* way."

"Yes, ma'am." McGurk sounded a bit crushed. But there was a determined glint in his eyes now. "By the way, does anyone around here have a grudge against you? Any enemies?"

Mrs. Pilsen shook her head.

"No. The police asked us that, right at the beginning."

"Sorry, McGurk!" said Merlin, smugly. "But it just *has* to be poltergeists!"

So we had to be content to leave it there for a while. Human perpetrators vs. poltergeists. Our reputation—our *proven* reputation—vs. the Weeping Wizard's *boasted* reputation.

But *some* person or persons—or spirit or spirits— didn't feel at *all* content to leave it there.

Because, the very next night, the dining room window was shattered again!

8 More Clues

McGurk received the news very early on Monday, the morning after the attack. It came in a phone call from Miss Pilsen. Luckily, there was no school that day.

It was clear and sparkling, and as McGurk told us about the call on the way to the Pilsen house, I felt a tingle of excitement. Somehow—I don't know why —it looked like it would be the kind of day when everything started to come together.

"I knew something had happened as soon as I heard Miss Pilsen's voice," McGurk began. "She sounded kind of strained—part annoyed, part scared. Anyway, she started by saying she was making the call at her aunt's request. Like she didn't want us to think *she* was calling for help."

"Why didn't Mrs. Pilsen herself call?" I asked.

"Miss Pilsen said the old lady was sick. In shock, I guess. Because of this latest attack. Sort of unexpected, even at *that* house."

"Yes, well, it surprised *me*," said Brains. "With the chicken wire still up and all. How did they bust through *that?* With a shotgun?"

"No. A rock. Like the other times. And when I asked her about the chicken wire she admitted it was her fault."

"How?"

"Well, the guy who'd fixed the new glass a few days before had smeared fingermarks around the edges. She didn't notice them at first, but when the sun shone on the glass she did. So early yesterday evening she took the chicken-wire screen down and started washing the window. Then she had to break off to see to something on the stove, and soon after that some visitor arrived and she clean forgot about it."

"Wow!" said Wanda. "I bet her aunt was mad!"

"I guess so," said McGurk. "But—"

He stopped. His freckles bunched up in a puzzled frown.

"What? What is it, McGurk?"

McGurk looked up. He blinked.

"Huh? . . . No. No, just something that struck me. Maybe it's nothing. Come on, men. We're wasting time."

After that, we couldn't get much else out of him, except that the attack had taken place at eight-thirty, and that the ladies were in one of the front rooms, talking with their visitor.

But he was excited, I could tell. Wanda must have sensed this, too. As McGurk strode forward, tight-lipped now, she nudged me and said, in a low voice:

"Looks like McGurk's got one of his hunches."

I nodded. "You bet!"

Anyway, just to give some idea of the crisp methodical way he tackled the next stage of the investigation, I'll break it down—step by step— and give each step a heading, like they do in the newspapers.

THE DAMAGE

Miss Pilsen answered the door. She looked pale and more disheveled than ever—like she'd slept in her clothes and hadn't even bothered to brush her hair. There were dark circles under her eyes, and her mouth was twitching.

"How is Mrs. Pilsen?" Wanda asked.

Miss Pilsen frowned.

"Resting!" she said, snappishly.

"Have the police been here yet, ma'am?" asked McGurk, getting down to business.

This seemed to suit Miss Pilsen's mood slightly better.

"No," she said, with a jerk of the head that seemed to direct her annoyance back inside the house. "My aunt wants to leave it strictly to *you*, this time."

McGurk had started to smirk. With Miss Pilsen's next words the smile disappeared.

"Strictly to you—and Merlin Snoegel."

But our leader's mood was too confident for him to be thrown for long.

"Sure! Could we see the damage, ma'am?"

"Certainly!" said Miss Pilsen, stepping out, then brushing past us as if we were nothing more than a bunch of dead leaves. "Follow me."

She led us into the back and stopped on the lawn opposite the dining room window.

McGurk grunted impatiently.

"Yes, ma'am. You told me over the phone it was this one. But . . . ."

He shrugged. The window had been boarded up already.

"But *what?* You asked to see the damage. There it is. A broken window is a broken window, after all."

"Yes, ma'am, but—well—where's the glass? Whereabouts was the hole—the—uh—"

"The center of the implosion," said Brains. "A lot can be learned from where the cracks are most numerous, the pattern made in spreading, the size and position of the broken bits, the *scatter* area."

"Yeah!" grunted McGurk. "All that."

Miss Pilsen stared angrily from McGurk to Brains and back.

"There was glass all over the place—as usual. My aunt was nearly in hysterics—as usual. My first concern was to sweep it all up and get the place as near to normal as possible. Quickly. It's in one of the garbage cans."

McGurk sighed.

"Yes. I understand, ma'am. But—uh—you did save the rock?"

"Yes. Also as usual. I suppose you'd like to see it?"

"Yes, please."

THE ROCK

I thought at first that it was a big potato she was holding when she returned. It had that dull sandy look.

THE ROCK

"It looks like the biggest yet," murmured McGurk, as he took it and turned it slowly in his hands.

"Oh, it is!" said Miss Pilsen. "It made us wonder what the next will be like."

"Don't worry, ma'am," said McGurk. He handed the rock to Brains. "There might not be a next!"

His eyes were gleaming.

"Oh?" murmured Miss Pilsen.

"One thing I can say right now," said Brains. "This isn't like any of the others. This is the sort you said sometimes crops up in the yard—right, ma'am?"

Miss Pilsen nodded. Her lips twitched into that uncertain smile again.

"Yes. That *is* a rather curious fact."

"Joey," said McGurk. "Note that down: *Rock could have come from Pilsen yard.*"

"Hey—come *on!*" Willie said to Brains.

He almost snatched the rock out of Brains's hands. Then he sniffed it.

"Anything?" McGurk asked.

Willie looked puzzled.

"That's another thing different. This one hardly smells of perfume at all. Just—mff! mff!—a trace."

"So what?" said Wanda. "You heard what Miss Pilsen said before. The smell comes from the drawer she keeps the rocks in. This one hasn't had time yet to pick up the smell—right?"

Willie nodded glumly. I felt sorry for him. It looked like his nose wasn't going to be much use to us in *this* case.

THE ROOM

"I'd still like to take a look inside the room itself," said McGurk.

The woman looked annoyed again.

"But what good will *that* do? I told you—I cleared the mess up last night."

"Yes, but maybe you could *show* us where the glass fell?"

Miss Pilsen sighed.

"Oh, well—my aunt did say you were to be given all the help you need. Personally, I think it's a sign of just how bad the poor dear is taking this. . . ."

It was gloomy in the dining room, with most of the window area boarded up. But it was light enough to see the general layout.

It was a large long room, made to seem smaller because of the furniture, heavy old dark brown stuff, with fancy twisted legs. The table ran lengthwise. There were three straight-backed chairs on each of the long sides. At the top and the bottom were bigger chairs, with arms.

Over against the wall opposite the window there was a huge sideboard.

But in spite of all this bulky furniture, there was still plenty of floor space. Between the table and the window, the distance must have been at least four feet.

Miss Pilsen told us about the glass.

"As before, there were big ugly slivers all over the table as well as the floor."

"Really, ma'am?" said Brains, frowning. "*Where* on the floor exactly?"

"Here," said Miss Pilsen, pointing to the spot just under the window with her foot. "And here . . . and here . . . *oh, all over!*"

"But *on* the table?"

"Yes! yes! How many more times do I have to tell you?"

"Sorry, ma'am—but, gosh! That rock must have been thrown with some force!"

Brains was looking awed.

"Where did you find the rock itself, Miss Pilsen?" Wanda asked.

"Oh, among the glass on the floor—under the table. I didn't notice it at first. But then—"

"*Elspeth!*"

The dry voice sounded faint. Probably it came from some room upstairs, I judged.

"Yes, Aunt, I'll be with you in a second!" Miss Pilsen called out. "Look," she said to us, "if you're through in here—"

"Yes, ma'am," said McGurk. "I guess there isn't much we could discover *now*. But I'd like to take another look around outside, if that's—"

"Of course! Of course!" said Miss Pilsen. "*Coming, Aunt!*" she called up the stairs, on the way through the hall. "But remember to keep your voices down!" she whispered savagely. "I think you must have woken her up!"

THE HEDGE

"Something wrong, Officer Bellingham?" said McGurk, as we stepped out into the sunlight.

"You mean in there?" said Brains. "Well . . . no. But the *force* of that missile!"

He shook his head.

"Forget about that for the time being," said Mc-

Gurk, looking all brisk and businesslike again. "Men, I want you to concentrate on the backyard."

"What are we looking for?" asked Willie.

"Clues. What else? Less than twenty-four hours ago, the perpetrators were *in* here. O.K., then. Let's see if they left anything—cigarette butts, candy wrappers, threads of cloth on the low branches there. Anything at all."

Well, we concentrated. But that yard was the neatest *I've* ever been in. There wasn't a scrap of paper anywhere, or threads of cloth, or cigarette butts, or even cigarette *ash*. None that we could find, anyway.

Meanwhile, McGurk prowled all the way around the hedge at the back, both inside and out of the yard. He did this especially carefully on the outside, getting us to join him, examining that hedge foot by foot.

"What are we looking for now, McGurk?" Willie asked.

"Same," grunted McGurk, probing and peering. "Clues. Signs of freshly broken twigs. That kind of thing."

He was very, very thoughtful. And unusually quiet. At every thinnish place—all those we'd checked out on Saturday—he stopped and probed and peered with extra care. Then he would shake his head, grunt, and move on.

And when we came to the place where Willie had first spotted Merlin, McGurk stopped for at least five minutes.

Finally, after peering through at every height and from every angle, he shook his head.

"Impossible!"

"What is?" said Wanda.

"To see anything inside there except the corner where the Wizard kid was standing. Check it out yourselves."

"If you're wondering how the perpetrator got in, McGurk," I said, "it must have been through the driveway. I thought we'd cleared that up on Saturday."

"Oh, *that!*" said McGurk, still scowling back at the last thin place as we moved away. "Yeah. I agree about *that.*"

"So—"

"So forget it for now. Let's see if Miss Pilsen can give us some more information."

THE INDEPENDENT WITNESS

"Well?" said Miss Pilsen, coming to the door. "Did you find anything?"

"No," said Wanda. "Except what we already knew. That whoever did it went in and out through the driveway entrance."

"Oh, but that's the big puzzle, young lady!" Miss Pilsen suddenly looked very uncomfortable—even scared. "You see, the Reverend Simpson was with us when it happened. Discussing—uh—poltergeists. And when the crash came he had the presence of mind to run out to the front—where all the flood-lights were on, incidentally. He told us later that he went out knowing exactly what he was doing—determined to block any attempt to escape."

McGurk nudged me.

"Note that down, Joey: *Independent witness.* Very important."

"Are you doubting my word, young man?"

"No, ma'am. Sorry! Just a routine note . . . . You were saying—about nobody getting out *that* way. But what if they hid in the yard until Mr. Simpson went back in the house?"

Miss Pilsen shook her head.

"No. You see, when Reverend Simpson ran out to the front, I went into the back. Grabbing the flash-light on my way. And I shone it all around the yard, in the trees, up the trees, everywhere."

McGurk was staring at her.

"And you found no one?"

"No one."

McGurk was looking *very* puzzled now.

POLTERGEISTS, AFTER ALL

"So it *does* look like poltergeists!" he muttered.

Brains gave a loud snort.

"What did Reverend Simpson say, ma'am?" he asked, pleadingly.

"Well, you'll be glad to know that he shares *your* view, young man. Partly, anyway. He believes there are such things—but not here. He says they've never been known to operate outside the walls of a building. In fact, he seemed convinced it was ordinary vandals."

Brains was looking very pleased. McGurk scowled.

"So all right, Officer Bellingham. How would *you* explain it?"

Path of Missile

Window

9 A New Possibility

Brains's grin broadened.

"Well, I've been thinking. It *would* be possible to break the window—any of the back windows—without stepping inside the yard. *Or* climbing the trees."

"How?" I said. "I mean, with a hedge *that* thick?"

"Sure! Lend me your notebook a minute and I'll show you."

Then, scribbling away rapidly, Brains drew the diagram shown above.

"There!" said Brains. "Like that. Up and over the hedge and the trees. Then down and—*bam!*"

Miss Pilsen winced.

"Hm!" muttered Wanda. "What about the rock? You said that this time the rock was picked up *inside* the yard."

"I only said it *could* have been. But it could also have come from anywhere nearby."

"The perpetrator would have to have a powerful arm," said McGurk. "Even a major-league pitcher—"

"Not if he used a slingshot," said Brains, tapping the diagram.

"Oh—that's what that Y thing is!" said McGurk. "Yeah. I see what you mean."

"Me, too!" said Willie. "So it could *still* be a slingshot sniper!"

"Come on!" said Wanda. "With rocks *this* size? Slingshots are only good for pebbles."

Brains nodded.

"Yes. Well. I've been thinking about that, too. I've been thinking it could have been a jumbo slingshot. The sort the Roman soldiers called a catapult. Big ones. Fired from the ground. Sometimes on wheels, to get them in and out of position quickly."

I must admit it was an interesting idea. A vivid picture flashed into my mind: the Four Flying Fingers dressed in Roman helmets and breastplates,

launching rocks at the Pilsen house with a powerful
catapult made from an old bicycle frame and a tire
inner-tube, mounted on a baby carriage.

Then I got serious.

"Yes," I said, "but *what* position? I mean this
would have to be precision work—pinpoint accuracy—to hit the target every time, first shot. It
would need a math genius."

"Well, yes!" said Brains. "That's what I was going
to say. And I know just the right person."

THE CONSULTANT

Miss Pilsen—who'd listened fascinated up until now at all the mention of snipers operating from the other side of the hedge—suddenly sighed, shook her head, and said she had to be getting on with her work indoors. McGurk hardly seemed to hear her, he was so interested in Brains's new theory.

"Who?"

Before Brains could answer, Wanda said:

"You're not thinking of Robinson Hackett, are you? Why would *he* want to break Mrs. Pilsen's windows?"

Brains was nodding.

"Yes! I *am* thinking of him. But not as a suspect. As a *consultant*."

"A what?" said Willie.

"Consultant," I said. "An adviser. Go on, Brains."

"Well, *I* don't know enough math to work out all the angles. But I bet Robinson Hackett could. He'd be able to tell us exactly where the missiles would have to be fired from. Also how heavy they'd have to be. Also how high over the trees they'd have to go to drop at just the right angle. Everything!"

McGurk had been looking doubtful. Terribly eager, but very doubtful.

"Yeah. But Robinson Hackett—he's a jerk!"

THE SPUR

Just then someone came scrunching along the driveway. Brains glanced back.

"Not as big a jerk as him!" he said, pointing to the newcomer, Merlin Snoegel. "And you were thinking of letting *him* be more than a consultant! You were thinking of letting *him* join the Organization! I could see it in your eyes!"

Merlin paused. His mouth flopped open in a sneery grin.

"Wasting the ladies' time again?" he said. "Haven't you learned your lesson yet? This is a job for an expert!"

That decided McGurk. That was the spur that made him get back into his brisk confident rhythm.

He glared at the Weeping Wizard. Maybe he'd suddenly realized how obnoxious Merlin would be if he *did* join us.

"You're right!" he said. "It *is* a job for an expert. A *math* expert . . . . Come on, men!"

10 Robinson Gets Interested

Brains was right about Robinson Hackett. Robinson is a math whiz. Both his parents are teachers—but they don't mind admitting that Robinson's math skills are way ahead of theirs. And that, for a thirteen-year-old, is pretty good.

McGurk, though, was not so right about Robinson. Sure, the kid was once jerk enough to try and make the Organization look like a bunch of dummies. But in the end it was we who made *him* look like a dummy. (As you'll know if you ever read *McGurk Gets Good and Mad.*) Now most kids would never have forgiven us for that. But old Robinson took it on the chin and came up smiling. Jerks don't usually do that.

In fact old Robinson took it on *both* chins. Because Robinson Hackett *is* fat. Fat and greedy. His greed caused him to trip up that time, when McGurk coaxed a confession out of him by tempting him with chocolate-covered peanuts.

We bought two packs of chocolate-covered peanuts on the way to Robinson's house that morning.

"He'll agree to help us out right away when he sees these," said McGurk.

Robinson himself came to the door. He was holding a book. I guessed at once he must have been deeply interested in it. He had that absent-minded look.

"Hi!" he said. "What brings *you* here?"

"Have some candy, Robinson," said McGurk, putting on his friendliest smile.

Robinson had worn a friendly smile, too, but when McGurk said that, he frowned.

"No, thanks. I'm dieting."

Willie gave him a closer look.

"Could have fooled *me!*"

"Be quiet!" said McGurk. Then he turned to Robinson. "Why, sure! I can see that now. You must have lost ten pounds since I last saw you."

Robinson looked pleased.

"Well, maybe not all that. But what I'm saying is I've sworn off candy and junk food. I eat sensible now." He held up the book so we could read the title: *French Provincial Cooking.* "*Gourmet* food. Just a little, but very delicious."

"What's goor-may?" asked Willie.

"A fancy foreign word," I said. "Meaning fancy foreign food."

"Take this dish, for instance," said Robinson, his mouth watering already as he opened the book. "Roast duckling with—"

"Yeah, yeah, sure!" said McGurk. "But we haven't come here to talk about food. We need your help. With a math problem. A practical math problem. To do with the case we're working on. Listen . . . ."

Then, very quickly, he told Robinson about the broken windows and Brains's latest theory.

"Show him Brains's drawing, Joey," he said at the end.

Robinson looked very critically at the diagram.

"It's just a very *rough* sketch," said Brains.

"You can say *that* again!" murmured Robinson. "No precision. No precision at all!" Then he looked up and all at once we breathed easier. His eyes were gleaming almost as brightly as McGurk's. "Well, sure—I'll help. It seems an interesting problem."

"Great!" said McGurk. "So where d'you think the rocks might have been fired from? How far? Which direction? Huh?"

Robinson was shaking his head.

"Not so fast! I'll need to know a lot more details."

"O.K. Like what?"

"Like the lay of the land around the Pilsen property. Especially at the back. It's ages since I was in that area."

"Sure! Joey—do you have that sketch-map you made yesterday?"

I nodded. After Mrs. Pilsen had sent us on our way on Saturday afternoon, there'd seemed to be nothing much left for us to do. But McGurk doesn't believe in wasting time when he's on a case, even if it seems to have gotten bogged down. So on Sunday he'd had us patrolling the Park Avenue North area—seeing if we could spot any *more* suspicious behavior. And then when that turned out to be a dead end, he had me draw this map:

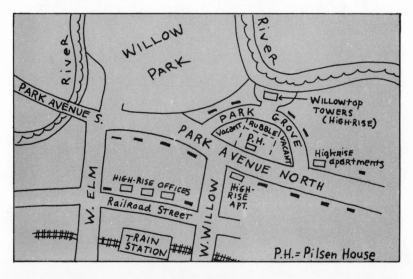

That is a copy I made since. The early notebook copy *was* a bit rough, I admit. Robinson gave it the same sort of look he'd given Brains's diagram.

"Hm! What are these black specks?"

"Just ranch houses," I said. "Or old ordinary-type houses."

"Hm! Well, from the look of *this*, I'd say the launching area could be anywhere inside this semicircle." He ran a pudgy finger over the area bounded by Park Grove. "Then again, it might be even farther back." He frowned at the map. "It's so imprecise. I need *exact* measurements."

"Well," said McGurk, glaring at me like it was *my* fault everything wasn't marked out to the nearest millimeter, "if you tell us what you—"

"No," said Robinson, giving my sketch another despairing glance. "I can see I shall have to supervise the measuring myself." He sniffed. His mouth was watering again. A faint smell of fried onions was coming through the open door. "But not before lunch!"

11 The Trial Shots

Right after lunch, Robinson Hackett joined us outside the Pilsen house. I guessed *his* lunch must have been very heavy, judging from the lazy glazed look in his eyes. But an expert soon wakes up when he starts to tackle a tricky technical problem, and Robinson was no exception.

Boy, was he no exception!

That guy had us working like beavers all afternoon. I mean, it wasn't enough for him to take a good long look around the Pilsen yard, the way McGurk had had us doing that morning.

Oh, no!

Robinson came loaded with a bunch of precision instruments he got from his father—a science teacher. Even Brains goggled at one of these, a thing that looked a bit like a telescope fixed to a brass wheel and mounted on a sort of camera tripod.

"A theodolite," Robinson explained. "To give us the *exact* height of the trees. And the *exact* heights of the windows."

"How?" asked McGurk.

Then Robinson went into a spiel about angles, and triangles, and fixed points, which only Brains came close to understanding. To the rest of us, it didn't seem much different from Merlin's wizard-type stuff.

But at least Robinson didn't go into a trance. In fact the more he worked on the problem, the wider awake he became, peering through the eyepiece, taking readings, and jotting them down in *his* notebook (much bigger than mine, with graph-paper pages).

"Hey, come on!" he said, looking up after a while. "There's work to be done. *You*—take the measuring tape and check the *exact* distance from the house wall to the foot of the hedge. *You*—give him a hand. *You* and *you*—take the other tape and measure the *exact* width of the yard. And *you*—take this measuring stick and get the *exact* height of the porch rails. And when you've done that . . . ."

And so on. Each *you* meaning a member of the Organization, including McGurk himself. I thought at first our leader would blow his top. But instead, with a shrug and a scowl, he turned to us.

"Come on! You heard what Robinson said! Get moving!"

So on it went, with Robinson checking and double-checking, jotting figures on his pad, frowning, stabbing away at a calculator, then jotting down more figures.

And at the end of the afternoon, he just laughed when McGurk said:

"So? How's it coming along, Robinson? Got all the details you need?"

"McGurk," said Robinson, "we've only just *started*. The next thing we need to do is construct a prototype—"

"A what?"

"A mock-up—a working model of a catapult. So that we can try it out for range and power. To see if such a thing would really *work*."

"Oh, boy!" said Brains, snatching off his glasses and polishing them. "Didn't I tell you Robinson was the tops, McGurk!"

So, the following day, after school (and in a way it was a relief that we did have to go back to school, a rest from Robinson's slave-driving!) we set to work in Brains's back yard making the prototype, with Robinson supervising.

We made it out of an old moveable TV stand, a bicycle chain, some cogwheels, and all kinds of other odds and ends, including an old rubber fan belt from a car. And when I say *we* made it, I guess I mean Robinson and Brains, with the rest of us running around looking for the bits and pieces.

Result—at the end of Tuesday afternoon—a really neat-looking contraption on wheels, with the top shelf now made adjustable to various slopes, and the thick rubber belt fixed so that it could be pulled back, close to the surface of the top shelf, and a handle and cogwheels arranged so that you could stretch the belt much further than if you did it with just your hands.

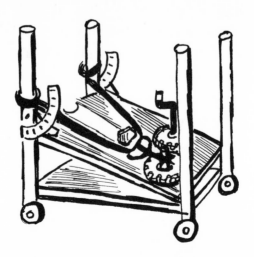

We tried it out with a rock in Brains's yard and—
wham!—we were lucky it didn't break one of the
Bellinghams' windows.

"There's power there, anyway," said Robinson.
"And range. But tomorrow we'll try it for accuracy."

"Can't we do that *now?*" pleaded McGurk.

"Not until I've worked out a precise set of tests.
Besides—uh—I'm hungry. . . ."

On Wednesday afternoon, Robinson decided to hold
the trials on the site at the back of the Pilsen house.
But again we were not allowed to get right into it.
No, sir!

"First we have to check the weights of all those
rocks," said Robinson. "Can you arrange it with the
Pilsen ladies, McGurk?"

McGurk frowned. Miss Pilsen had already shown
signs of being totally fed up with us on Monday
afternoon, when we'd been doing all the measuring.
But Mrs. Pilsen was up and about again, and
although she still looked very pale and worried, she
said of *course* we could weigh the rocks.

Robinson had brought his own scales. "Precision-
tested," he explained, and after weighing and re-
weighing and weighing the rocks still again, he

studied the figures he'd jotted down and seemed satisfied.

Then he led the way back to the mock-up catapult, which we'd left between the heaps of rubble, with Willie on guard.

"Did you see Merlin?" Willie asked.

"No, why?"

"Oh, nothing! It's just that he's been mooching around, weeping again. He says even if it isn't polter-whatsits and it was living people, he bets he can find the spot where the rocks were fired from. He says he'll be able to feel the vibrations."

"Forget him!" said Brains. "This is the only way we'll find the launching site. By accurate scientific tests. Right, Robinson?"

"Right. So why don't you all get busy and find me a rock weighing as close to sixteen ounces as possible."

When we'd gathered a heap of likely rocks, and he'd weighed them and selected five, he said:

"Now for the test shots."

He fitted one of the rocks in place, cranked back the rubber and pointed the trolley to a huge heap of timber.

"First, to check the elevation, we'll call that heap

a fairly high hedge. I'll increase the slope of the launcher—so—and now we shall see how easily we can clear the barrier."

Well, what we saw was the rock hurtling high in the air, all right. And had Robinson been as good at aiming as he was at calculating, it would have cleared the top of the heap by about four feet.

But it was too far to one side—and maybe that was just as well. Because right then, who should come from behind the heap—slowly turning and turning, and bowing, and weeping—but Merlin.

The rock landed a couple of paces away from him, hitting a hunk of corrugated iron. Merlin must have been deep in one of his trances. The noise made him leap like he'd been stung, and he ended up falling on his backside.

He turned his head toward us. His eyes blazed through the tears.

"You did that on purpose!" he howled.

"Honestly, we didn't!" said Wanda, starting over to help him up.

"Don't touch me!" he said, getting up by himself. "I'll cast a spell on your lousy Organization now! You see if I don't!"

"Baloney!" said Brains, as the Wizard stalked away.

"Hey! We're sorry!" McGurk called out, looking worried. "We didn't know you were—"

"You're wasting time," said Robinson. "Take a hold of this end of the measuring tape."

We soon forgot the incident. By now we'd all got the feeling that Robinson's calculations were coming to a head. So we worked with real enthusiasm on the rest of the trial shots. And when Robinson sat down amid the rubble and began drawing careful curves on his graph paper, we were silent.

"All rightee!" he said at last. "I think I can now say, McGurk, that young Brains's theory is perfectly sound. The targets *could* have been hit in this way. Here, take a look."

We clustered around the diagram. Here's a copy of it:

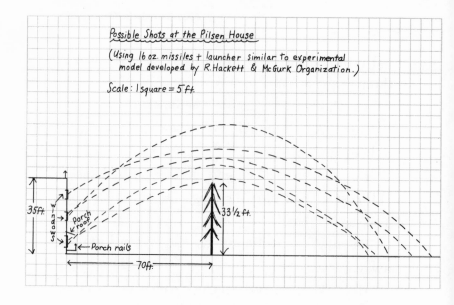

Possible Shots at the Pilsen House

(Using 16 oz. missiles + launcher similar to experimental model developed by R. Hackett & McGurk Organization.)

Scale: 1 square = 5 ft.

35 ft.

Windows

Porch roof

← Porch rails

33½ ft.

70 ft.

"As you'll see," said Robinson, "I've selected just one end of the house. I've also selected just one weight of rock. But it shows that it can be done."

McGurk was staring like he'd been hypnotized. Several times his lips moved, ready to speak, but then closed tight again.

"So does this tell us the exact spot the rocks *were* launched from?" I asked.

Robinson shook his head.

"No. This is just a guide. With a machine like this—well—the actual launching site could be—well—anywhere within several hundred feet. Depending on the strength and design of the actual machine."

McGurk was still staring at the diagram—seeming to gaze right through it.

"Oh, boy!" said Wanda. "You mean to say that after all this work—"

"Some more work is still needed?" said Robinson. "Yes. . . . But don't worry. We're getting there."

He looked around slowly, from the trees at the back of the Pilsen house, across to the ranch houses along the opposite side of Park Grove and the trees there, and even as far as the Willowtop Towers high-rise building beyond.

"Getting where?" said Willie.

"Don't forget," said Robinson, ignoring the question, "the launching site doesn't have to be at ground level. It could be the roof of one of those houses. Or the top of a shed. Or on a pile of something, like around here. It could even be in a pit of some kind, concealed in one of those ranch house yards."

"So what do you suggest?" I asked sarcastically. "A house-to-house search?"

I glanced at McGurk. Still in a trance.

"Not necessarily," said Robinson. "If I could get a look at the area from a high enough point—"

"How about a helicopter?" said Wanda.

Even Brains was looking disappointed.

"Or a satellite?" he said.

Robinson was smirking.

"What I had in mind was something much more simple. Like a high enough building. Like that one there."

"The Willowtop Towers?" said Wanda. "Why—do you know someone who lives there?"

"No." Robinson's fat cheeks were glowing and his lips were glistening. "But there's a public restaurant on the thirtieth floor. The Willowtop Lodge. And if you could arrange for us to have a—uh—little snack up there, McGurk, I'm sure I'd be able to put the finishing touches to our research program."

Wanda gasped. So did I.

The Willowtop Lodge restaurant was one of the best in town. And the most expensive. Had Robinson Hackett been working up to this all along? A free meal, at the Organization's expense?

McGurk's gaze was now aimed at Robinson. I got ready for the explosion.

But:

"Sure," he said, still kind of dreamily. "Good idea, Robinson. We'll do that. We have over seventy dollars in the treasury, don't we?"

"Yes," I said. "But—"

"So make the reservations. O.K.?"

Then he turned back to the diagram, leaving Robinson beaming and the rest of us looking at each other with a mix of amazement and anxiety.

Had McGurk lost his marbles?

Did he know what he was doing?

Was the Weeping Wizard casting his spell already?

12 "Which One Is the Slingshot Sniper?"

When I called the Willowtop Lodge restaurant that afternoon, the first thing they asked was if I was a kid. And when I said yes, they said they didn't accept reservations from kids. In fact kids weren't even allowed in the restaurant unless accompanied by an adult.

"So all right," said McGurk, "we'll get an adult to take us. If we tell him or her *we're* paying, they'll be glad of the chance."

Well, as soon as we started wondering which adult, we realized that that wasn't going to be easy, either. A parent? A neighbor?

"And what would we tell them?" I asked. "How would we explain, without going into details?"

McGurk frowned. He hates discussing unfinished cases with outsiders.

Then Wanda had her great idea.

"I suppose it wouldn't matter going into details with the Pilsen ladies. After all, it *is* their case."

At first when we put the proposition to Miss Pilsen it didn't seem like such a great idea.

As soon as McGurk mentioned the Willowtop Lodge restaurant, she looked shocked. Then she blushed, like maybe she thought we were making fun of her.

"Why? What do you want to go *there* for?"

But when McGurk explained that it was the only place for Robinson to check out the possible sites for the giant slingshot, she simmered down.

"Well, it *is* expensive. I've been there a few times myself and—"

"That's O.K., Miss Pilsen," said McGurk. "We don't eat much when we're on an investigation. But *you* could order what you liked. Our treat, of course."

We'd been standing at the Pilsen front door. And again, from somewhere inside, came Mrs. Pilsen's dry voice:

"That sounds reasonable, Elspeth. I shan't be able to go, but you must. And, since it's in our interest, I don't see why we shouldn't pay. So long as it doesn't come to more than—uh—seventy-five dollars."

"Gee, thanks, ma'am!"

Then Mrs. Pilsen took an even bigger load off the minds of some of us.

"Furthermore, if any of your parents should wonder what this meal is all about, you can tell them it's a reward. For working so hard on our problem. Ask them to call me if they wish to check."

"Terrific!" said McGurk.

The voice got even dryer.

"Anything *over* seventy-five dollars, mind, you'll have to pay for yourselves."

So that's how we came to visit one of the town's ritziest restaurants, late the following afternoon. We were all in our best clothes. As for Miss Pilsen, we hardly recognized her when we met her in the Willowtop Towers lobby.

She was wearing a very neat lavender-blue suit. She even looked like she'd had her hair done for the occasion. And when we were going up in the elevator and she started fishing about in her purse, we were nearly overpowered with her perfume.

"I must make sure I've brought my credit cards," she said, giggling nervously. "I always—why, what's the matter?"

Poor Willie looked like he was going to faint. What was overpowering to our ordinary noses must have been almost *lethal* to his.

"No—nothing!" he mumbled. "Just the lily of the—um—valley scent again."

"Oh, yes—that! I'm afraid a bottle once broke inside my purse. I'm so used to it now I hardly notice it."

We were all glad when we reached the thirtieth floor. Then we forgot about the perfume, we were so busy looking around.

At first I thought we'd made a mistake and had gotten out at a floor full of offices. On the corridor wall, just in front of the elevator, was a bunch of signs:

K. R. Realty Inc.
Kurt Ritschard Development Inc.
Kurt Ritschard Associates Inc.
Ritschard Property Management Inc.
K. R. Hunting Lodges Inc.
K. R. Restaurants Inc.

There was a big arrow at the bottom, pointing to the right.

"Come *on*, Officer Rockaway!" said McGurk.

Then I realized the others were already heading left and going through some swinging doors, where there were lots of dark green plants, and when I followed it was like stepping into another world.

I mean—all right—so this was a restaurant. I could see that. But what made me gape—what made us all gape—was the way it was decorated.

Like for instance the stuffed animal heads stuck on the walls. Most had horns: straight horns, branched horns, curly twisted horns. And if they didn't have horns, they had tusks.

"Wow!" gasped Willie.

"I wish they'd been satisfied with the shields!" Wanda murmured. "Now they *are* decorative."

Between the heads were clusters of little colored shields. And under the shields, crossed and fixed to the walls, were spears and lances and daggers and powder horns and muskets and carbines and rifles and—

"Welcome to the Willowtop Lodge!" said a fat lady, dressed like a Swiss peasant, and she led us to a table over to one side.

At first I thought she was putting us out of the way because we were a bunch of kids. It wasn't very busy and there were plenty of free tables by the long windows straight ahead, all with a beautiful view of Willow Park. But I guess Miss Pilsen must have asked especially for our table, because this one had a view of the town, stretching into the distance, with the Park Avenue area just below us.

"Perfect!" said McGurk.

Then Miss Pilsen said, "Now where shall we all sit?" and we had to remember our manners and settle down and pretend to be interested in the big menu cards.

Some of us had to pretend, anyway. But Robinson —our technical consultant—the guy we were *doing* all this for—didn't have to. No way! That guy settled down to the lists of dishes like he was all set for a good long read of a very thrilling adventure story.

Then McGurk caught his breath like *he'd* just reached the scariest part of a horror story.

"Hey!" he whispered. "Look at these *prices!*"

Just then the waiter came up. He was dressed like a Swiss peasant, too—with little green leather shorts, white socks, buckled shoes, a frilly shirt, and a little green hat with a feather in it.

Even this sight couldn't draw our leader's eyes away from those prices.

"Now then, what shall we have?" said Miss Pilsen, brightly.

"Well . . . ."

"Uh . . . ."

"Maybe . . . ."

"I wonder if . . . ."

McGurk made up his officers' minds for them.

"The Organization will have hamburgers and

french fries!" He scowled around. "With plain water.
We need to keep our heads clear, men!"

I glanced at the menu. He'd picked the cheapest,
sure enough, but even that was going to make a big
hole in the seventy-five-dollar limit.

Robinson suddenly looked up. His expression was
pained.

"Personally, I don't much care for hamburgers.
Especially when—"

"No, that's O.K., Robinson," said McGurk. "That
order's just for the officers and me. You pick what
you want. Within reason!"

So Robinson and Miss Pilsen went into a big number about what looked good, and what was fresh—

ending with Miss Pilsen showing mercy on McGurk and simply ordering soup and an omelet. Robinson, however, had to have another long chat—this time with the waiter. And in the end he ordered some of the most expensive items on the list. (Which I looked up later, to get the spellings right.)

"I'll have the *escargots* to start with, I think. . . . Yes. And—um—yes—the *caille flambée*. With the *pommes fondantes*, of course. And—why not?—just a few of the *topinambours à la provençale*."

McGurk was nearly going cross-eyed trying to track these items down and see how much they cost. I'd already worked it out roughly at twenty-five dollars minimum. So maybe it was just as well that the stranger walked up to the table just then, greeted Miss Pilsen, and said something that took us right back to the heart of the mystery:

"Which one of you is the Slingshot Sniper?"

13 Snails and Quails

We stared at the stranger.

He wasn't tall, but he had broad, powerful shoulders. His hair was silvery gray, cut short, but his tanned face looked fairly young. His eyes were very sharp, clear and blue. He wore a smooth dark gray suit.

Other people were looking at him, too—customers, waiters, and the woman in the peasant dress.

Then we realized why.

"This is Mr. Ritschard," said Miss Pilsen. Her eyes were shining and her smile was wobbling like crazy. "He owns the restaurant."

He smiled, showing a lot of gold. Remembering the

notices by the elevator, I expected him to say, "Yes, and I own a few more things besides!"

But instead he said:

"How do you like it? I tried to get it to look like a genuine hunting lodge."

He waved at the animals' heads and the spears and badges.

"Like a real hunting lodge in the Swiss Alps," said Miss Pilsen, blushing. "Where Mr. Ritschard comes from."

"Did those heads belong to real animals?" Wanda asked.

"Indeed they did!" Mr. Ritschard didn't seem to notice Wanda's accusing stare. "Why, some of them I shot myself. Like the ibex there and—"

"Oh, dear!" said Miss Pilsen. "I'm sorry, but I always feel squeamish when I think of the poor hunted animals."

Mr. Ritschard didn't seem to like that. He frowned. But then McGurk chipped in.

"Excuse me, sir. What did you mean when you asked which one of us was the Slingshot Sniper?"

The man laughed.

"Just my little joke!" Then his face went serious. "But Miss Pilsen tells me one of you had a brilliant idea to solve her problem. About a giant slingshot."

Brains put up his hand.

"Yes, sir! Me, sir! I did!"

Then he went on to explain how we'd made a mock-up catapult and had Robinson working out the calculations.

"Hm!" murmured Mr. Ritschard. "Well, I must say you seem to be on the right track." He went to the window. "Something like that could very well have been used. Yes, indeed!"

Naturally, we were quick to get up and crowd around him. From where we were, we could see the Pilsen property clearly. We could even see over the trees to where the sun was glowing on all the back windows.

"Now it seems to me," said Mr. Ritschard, "that there are several vantage points where the catapult could have been placed. Even as far away as those houses on Park Grove."

"Yes, sir!" said Robinson. "It's just a question of deciding whether one fixed point was used, or if the machine was moved from place to place."

"Good!" said Mr. Ritschard. "Good thorough thinking. It's the only way to deal with really difficult problems. . . ." He straightened up and turned. "But—ah!—I see your food is ready. Busy heads can't work efficiently on empty stomachs!"

Then he bowed to Miss Pilsen, peered at the dishes in the waiter's hands, and left us.

Well, Miss Pilsen's first course was soup—and soup is soup. The Organization's first nibbles were at the freebies—the rolls and sticks of celery and bits of carrot—and there's no big deal about *them*, either.

But what made us forget even the view was Robinson's food.

It came on two plates, an ordinary big dinner plate with a smaller metal plate on top. In the metal plate were six holes, and in each hole something was sizzling, with a topping of melted butter and bits of greenery. Along with the plate came a kind of round-nosed silver pincers, like a miniature ice cream scoop, and a small thin fork.

Robinson sniffed the aroma, beamed, put the pincers in one of the holes, and pulled out something hard and brown. Then he stuck the fork into this shell and pulled out something soft and gray and squishy. Then he popped it in his mouth and munched happily.

"Delicious!" he murmured, dipping a piece of bread into the hole. "Absolutely delicious!"

"What is it, Robinson?" Wanda asked.

"Escargots," he said, dropping the empty shell

onto the bottom plate. "Escargots in garlic butter."
He grinned. "You know: snails."

Five pairs of eyes looked quickly away from his
plates. Someone gulped noisily. Someone else nearly
choked.

"I wish I'd never asked!" said Wanda.

For once she spoke for every single member of the
Organization.

However, by the time they'd cleared away Robinson's and Miss Pilsen's plates, we were beginning to
feel better. And when the hamburgers and french
fries arrived, we were ready to tackle them. Miss
Pilsen's omelet didn't look bad, either.

But before we could start, we had to wait for
Robinson's second course to appear—and when it
did we saw why it had to be brought on its own.

"Hey! It's on fire!" cried Willie, getting to his feet.

"Sit down!" said Robinson. "It's *supposed* to be."

He beamed again as the waiter set down the big oval silver plate. Under the flickering flames were several pieces of what looked like charred toast. His costly vegetables were placed in separate dishes at the side, but we only had eyes for the main dish. Even before the flames had gone out, Robinson was spearing one of the blackened pieces on his fork.

"Why!" said Wanda. "They're like little shriveled-up birds! I can see a pair of little legs! They—they're *sparrows!*"

"They *are* birds," said Robinson, munching blissfully. "Only they're *quails*, not sparrows."

"Disgusting!" said Wanda. "First he eats broiled slugs, now this!"

She was sitting between me and McGurk. And at the words "broiled slugs," I heard our leader's chair scrape back.

"Excuse me!" he muttered.

He walked to the window and pressed his forehead against the glass, staring out.

"You shouldn't have said that about the slugs," said Willie.

"I'm sorry!" said Wanda. "Are you all right, Mc-Gurk?"

He didn't reply. Miss Pilsen looked worried. I got up and went to his side.

"You O.K.?"

He nodded. He was staring down in the direction of the Pilsen house through the faint mist his breath was making on the glass. His face was pale. His eyes were gleaming, like he was concentrating. Fighting hard to take his mind off Wanda's words, I guessed.

"Look!" said Robinson, getting up. "You shouldn't take any notice of her. These were specially culti-vated snails—"

"Robinson," said McGurk, turning glassy eyes on our math consultant, "forget it. Go back and enjoy your burnt birds. . . . Joey, would you mind coming with me to the men's room?"

I went with him, holding onto him with one hand, hoping he'd make it in time.

But when he got there he didn't head straight for a cubicle or go to one of the sinks. No. He went in-stead to the end window and looked out.

"Good!" he said. "It's the same side. See, Officer Rockaway? The Pilsen house again!"

He still looked pale.

"Don't you think you'll feel better with a splash of cold water?" I asked.

He turned and blinked.

"Water? Why water?" Then he snapped his fingers. "Do you have a dime?"

"Well—uh—yes. Sure!"

"Let me have it. I think I saw a pay phone in the corridor outside."

He was right. I followed him to it. I watched as he flipped through the directory, then found the

number he wanted. I was still wondering about his mental state when someone answered.

"Hi, Mrs. Pilsen!" he said, in a low but eager voice. "It's me—Jack P. McGurk. Can I ask you one question? . . . Yes. It *is* important. . . . Has anyone tried to buy your house recently? . . . Really? And when did they first make the offer? . . . As long ago as *that*, huh? Well, thank you very much! You've helped me solve the mystery."

I must have gasped, because he turned and shushed me sharply.

"No. It's very complicated," he went on, into the phone. "I need to work out the details. But tomorrow —after school—say three-thirty, I'll present them to you, with all the facts and all the witnesses. Plus one of the chief perpetrators. . . . We'll be there, ma'am, don't worry!"

He didn't say anything else to her. As for me—one of his principal officers and oldest friend—all he'd say was:

"You heard what I told her. I have to work out a few details yet."

Then we went back to the others, and he was so pleased he allowed the Organization to finish with ice cream. He didn't even wince when Robinson chose a massive hunk of Black Forest cake, studded with cherries and dripping with whipped cream. He even went through the motions of looking out of the window with Robinson afterward, and pointing out likely sites for the giant slingshot.

But I could tell he wasn't really interested in that angle any more. I could also tell that it was no use asking him again what angle he *had* seized on.

With McGurk in one of his secretive moods— saving it all up for his Big Showdown scene—I knew we'd just have to wait.

All I hoped was that he knew what he was doing!

14 The Big Showdown

"Right from the start, things didn't add up right."

That's how McGurk began, the following afternoon, at approximately three thirty-five.

The place: the Pilsen dining room.

Those present: McGurk himself, at one end of the table; the Pilsen ladies at the opposite end; the rest of the McGurk Organization; the Four Flying Fingers; Merlin Snoegel; and Robinson Hackett.

Extra chairs had been brought in.

McGurk was wearing his best suit again. Mrs. Pilsen looked thinner than ever. Miss Pilsen had gone back to her usual sloppy clothes and already her hair was starting to look untidy.

The rest of the Organization had flatly refused to wear their best clothes. Like Wanda said:

"If you won't tell us beforehand exactly who your prime suspect is, McGurk, I for one am not getting dressed up for your big scene!"

She was right about the "big scene." McGurk had always longed for something like this. Where the Big Detective gets everybody into one room at the end, suspects and helpers alike. With even the helpers having to wait for his words! Even the guys who did all the legwork and more than a little of the brainwork, too! The jerk!

Anyway, at least we'd tidied ourselves up. So had the four little kids. McGurk had warned them that it would look bad for them if they didn't.

"Because you're *still* suspects!" he'd said.

So there they sat, looking a bit scared, but cleaner than I'd ever seen them.

Merlin was in his black sweater, lolling back and trying to look unconcerned. But he was taking in every word McGurk uttered.

Robinson was looking a bit dreamy. I guess he was wondering what there'd be for supper.

But back to McGurk . . . .

"First there was the question: How did the per-petrators get in?" He looked around, then focused a fierce glare on the Fingers. "Gaps in the hedge? No way. We checked that. We checked for gaps that could be used by even the littlest kids."

McGurk leaned forward and stabbed a finger at Sam.

"Tell us," said McGurk, "in your own words, just what happened when you decided to get those pine cones."

"We saw these trees," said Sam, nervously. "Pine trees. We figured there'd be lots of cones under them. We figured we'd tidy up for the ladies—"

"Answer the question!"

"Uh—well—then we tried to get in through the hedge. We couldn't. Not even Lonny here—he's the skinniest. So—well—we just went around to the front and snuck in through the driveway."

"O.K.," said McGurk. He went back to addressing the whole meeting. "So next there was the spook theory. Evil spirits. Poltergeists." McGurk turned to the Weeping Wizard. "So that brought Merlin on the scene."

Merlin closed his eyes.

"I still think—," he began, in his trance voice.

"Evil spirits?" said McGurk. "I agree." Merlin's eyes snapped open. "But not the kind *you* had in mind."

"What kind do you have in mind then?" said
Merlin.

"I'll be coming to that. . . . Anyway, that brings
me to the next solid clue—the *visibility* angle. It
began to worry me the day we first spotted Merlin
in the yard." McGurk glanced around. "There was
only *one* place in the hedge—one slight gap—we

could see him from. When he was standing down there at the end of the yard," he added. "Remember, men?"

One by one, as those fierce green eyes met ours, we nodded, wondering what he was getting at.

"Only Officer Sandowsky, in that one place, got a look at Merlin. At the other end of the yard . . . ."

"So?" Wanda sounded impatient.

"So I remembered that later. When someone took advantage of the fact that the chicken wire was down—from just one window—for just a few hours."

"Are you suggesting—?" Mrs. Pilsen began.

But even she couldn't stop our leader.

"Excuse me, ma'am. It'll be clear very soon. . . . So then I asked myself: Who could *know* about the chicken wire being down? Who'd be able to see it from outside the yard? And I checked again. And there was not one single gap where you can see the windows from!"

"They—" Miss Pilsen cleared her throat. "The rock-throwers must have been *in* the yard then."

"You mean someone snuck in during *daylight*, ma'am? Just to check on the chicken wire? . . . Risky, wasn't it? When for all they knew the wire might be up for weeks, like before?"

Miss Pilsen flushed.

"Well then—*after* dark. When—when they smashed the window."

McGurk pounced.

"But that's when you and Mr. Simpson made sure nobody *could* have been inside!"

Miss Pilsen shrugged. She glanced at her aunt.

"Oh well, if you really want to know, I *still* think it's poltergeists."

"Or Evil Forces," said Mrs. Pilsen. "I'm beginning to feel *that*, even more. Go on, young man."

Brains was muttering. McGurk glared at him.

"Or some way of projecting the rocks from outside the yard. Don't forget *that*, ma'am. Officer Bellingham's theory. Proved possible with Robinson Hackett's expert help. A really smart piece of work."

Brains and Robinson looked very pleased.

I said:

"But it still means the person who fired the catapult had to know about the chicken wire."

"Sure! But we'll let that rest for the time being. The point is that the catapult method was possible. *But*—," he smiled his mysterious smile—"but *possible* isn't the same as *likely*. Never forget that, men."

"Go on!" said Wanda.

McGurk's eyes were shining.

"I mean it took a math whiz to work out the possibility. O.K.? So it would take *another* math whiz to put it into practice. To aim that thing with one hundred per cent accuracy every time. One rock, one hit."

"I guess he could fire off a few rocks *before* hitting the target," said Brains.

"Maybe. But I doubt it. The ladies would have heard any near-misses—any rocks hitting the shingles."

"Yes, indeed," said Mrs. Pilsen. "But there was always just the one crash. Of glass."

"Right," said McGurk. "And another thing. There'd be marks on the paint. Scars and dents. But there aren't any."

Everyone was silent now. Miss Pilsen's mouth opened, but she didn't speak.

"So what it began to look like," said McGurk, "was that this was an *inside job!*"

There was a murmur. Then Miss Pilsen found her voice. It came out fiercely, rising to a squeak.

"What do you *mean?*"

"I mean that someone inside the house was doing it. Or helping to do it. Faking it to look like vandalism. Or poltergeists."

All eyes were on the two ladies now. Mrs. Pilsen

sat very still, very stiff, very upright. Miss Pilsen squirmed.

"Rubbish! There's only my aunt and myself here. Why should we—?"

"That's what puzzled me, ma'am. Insurance money? No point. Some sort of publicity stunt? Wanting to see your names in the paper?"

"I've never heard of such nonsense!" said Mrs. Pilsen.

"It happens, ma'am. But not with ladies like you. It's usually half-crazy show-offs. They'll even confess to crimes they haven't committed. So—," Mc-Gurk shook his head—"*that* didn't seem to be the motive, either."

"Anyway," said Miss Pilsen, "whatever the motive, how could either of us do it without the other one knowing? We were always together when the crash happened."

"Right! Good question, ma'am! I asked myself that. Which took me back to the possibility of outsiders. And that other big question: How so accurate every time? It baffled me. I looked at Robinson's diagram again and again. But it wasn't until we went to the Willowtop Lodge place that something happened to—"

"I know!" said Robinson. "When you saw the

view from above." Then he frowned. "But how did that help?"

"It didn't. Not at first. First I had to be put on the right track. And *that* only happened when you ordered your snails."

"My—*escargots?*"

"Yeah. To be exact, it was when Wanda called them *slugs. Then* it hit me. *Then* I saw how it could have been done. Simple. Direct. With a *rifle* slug. A bullet."

He pulled out a piece of yellow paper, unfolded it, and held it up. It was Robinson's diagram—with one difference. A straight bright line in red ink had been added. Like this:

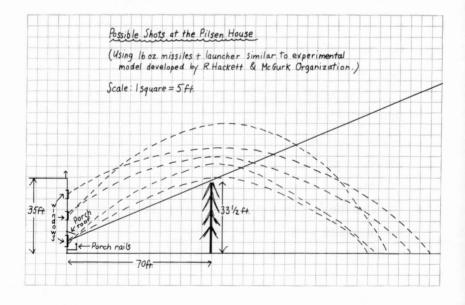

Possible Shots at the Pilsen House

(Using 16 oz. missiles + launcher similar to experimental model developed by R. Hackett & McGurk Organization.)

Scale: 1 square = 5 ft.

35 ft.
windows
Porch roof
← Porch rails
33 ½ ft.
70 ft.

"Of course, three things were still needed to complete the picture," said McGurk. "One: a good place to shoot from, with a clear view of all these windows. Two: a crack shot. And three: a motive." He paused. Then he pointed out of the recently mended window. "And there they were! In the Willowtop Towers itself!"

"You—you mean Mr. Ritschard?"

Wanda's voice was very respectful.

"Yes. The guy who's such a great marksman with a hunting rifle. Also the guy who owns the company that wants to build a high-rise apartment building right here—if only Mrs. Pilsen will sell this house so he can tear it down."

Dead silence. Then McGurk faked an apologetic look.

"But I forgot. One *more* thing was needed."

"What?"

"An accomplice. Someone to plant the rocks among the broken glass."

We all turned to look at Miss Pilsen. Now *she* had become very still.

"But wouldn't the glass show the bullet hole?" said Brains. "And wouldn't the slug embed itself in the furniture or the floor? Or just lie around someplace?"

"Not if the accomplice found it first. As to the hole, it could have been a dum-dum bullet. The sort that spreads as soon as it hits, and then makes a hole like a rock. In any case, when you see a rock in a mess of broken glass, who thinks of bullets?"

"*I* certainly didn't!" said Mrs. Pilsen, in a voice as dry as gunpowder.

"Anyway," said McGurk, "after that, everything fit. Including the scent, Officer Sandowsky. *You* were on the right track."

"Wu—was I?"

"Sure. Like when you noticed the last rock hardly smelled at all. And why?"

"Uh—not inside the box long enough?"

"No! Because the smell inside Miss Pilsen's purse was very powerful. And *that's* where the earlier rocks had picked it up. Not from the box. Not the drawer."

"This is absurd!" said Miss Pilsen.

In the last few minutes her hair seemed to have become completely messed up.

"No, ma'am. It makes good sense. You brought the rocks in from all over, mainly out in the vacant lots. Hidden in your purse. Except for the last one. Which you found in the yard—to help boost the poltergeist theory!"

"All very clever," said Mrs. Pilsen, still without looking at her niece. "But I can't help thinking that at least one bullet might have gotten itself embedded *somewhere.*"

"Very likely, ma'am. The police will probably want to check the floorboards. Maybe even the outside walls, too, because a bullet missing a window probably wouldn't make as much noise as a rock. But—*Joey! Wanda! Stop her!*"

Miss Pilsen was heading for the door like she'd been shot from a catapult herself.

15 Full Confession

Wanda and I were nearest the door, but we didn't have to do anything. From that moment, Mrs. Pilsen took charge.

"Let her be! She's only going to pack."

"But, ma'am—"

"And when she's done *that*, she's going to give me a full confession!"

The old lady sounded grim, like she was adding, "If she knows what's good for her!"

Anyway, that was the end of the case for us. The rest was up to Mrs. Pilsen—and the police.

Our original clients were very satisfied. All smiles.

"Not bad, McGurk!" said Sam. "It took you long enough. But—not bad!"

There was just one problem. About the fee.

"We spent it," said Sam, when they came to settle up a few days later. "We had to *live*, while you were taking all that time. But here—take these. They're worth more than three dollars and fifteen cents."

"These" were two big garbage sacks stuffed with pine cones!

Our other client was just the opposite. Mrs. Pilsen did pay us in cash, the next day. Twenty-eight fifty. "To cover your extra expenses at the restaurant." But no smiles.

Still grim, and sort of sad, she said:

"I suppose you've a right to know what I managed to get out of my niece. . . . Well, she confessed everything. She'd been betraying me all those months, but she said she really thought it was for my own good. The money Ritschard was offering for the house *was* a very large sum."

She sighed.

"That, in fact, was one of the reasons the scoundrel got her to go along with him in the plot. The other reason—well—she's a poor foolish woman, and I guess he flattered her a lot. She thought he was wonderful."

"Yes," said Wanda. "I could see that at the restaurant."

"I'd started to suspect *something* of the sort," said Mrs. Pilsen. "But I couldn't for the life of me see how it was being done. Until you came along."

"Sure!" said McGurk, *very* smugly.

"It could have been dangerous," I said. "Using a rifle."

"I told her that," said Mrs. Pilsen. "But she said no. They'd arranged for him to shoot only at the window of a room which Elspeth made sure was vacated. Starting with the attic windows, where we very rarely go anyway. And, to make it all simpler, she'd usually put the light on in the target room."

"Yeah, but something could have gone wrong!" said McGurk, serious again. "He could have had a cramp in his arm. Or some bug could have bitten him while he was squeezing the trigger. Then— *bam!*—some innocent person could have been hit."

"Reckless endangerment!" I said.

"I know," said Mrs. Pilsen. "That's why I *had* to bring in the police. And indeed, they have found a slug. Embedded in a dark corner under the sill of one of the attic windows. . . . Besides," she went on, "while Elspeth's treachery was bad, the man's using her like that was downright criminally evil. *Encouraging* her to be a traitor!"

The dry voice was shaking with anger.

"Anyway, I think she'll get off lightly. I shall certainly speak up for her in court. And of course she'll be able to come back here, if she wishes."

"What about him?"

"Well, *he'll* get all he deserves. And that could be a stiff prison sentence. In any event, he won't be troubling *us* again."

McGurk was satisfied. After all, it *had* been one of his biggest triumphs. He even had another good word for Merlin, back at our HQ.

"You know, men, that old Weeping Wizard—he really *was* on the right track. He got the sense of something—uh—evil, didn't he? All he needed was a good detective brain to guide him. In fact—yeah, why not?—we'll keep him in mind in the future."

"Oh, *no!*" howled Brains. "You're not thinking of making him a *member?*"

"Well . . . maybe just a consultant."

Obviously the idea was still attractive to him. Just as it was obnoxious to the rest of us.

But there's no arguing with McGurk. So, to change the subject, I said:

"Anyway, McGurk, I've thought of a new addition to the notice. To the list of things we do."

"Yeah? What?"

"This," I said, showing him the neat typing job I'd already done:

```
SNIPERS   SNARED

      &

TRAITORS   TRAPPED
```

He liked that. Loved it.

I'm only hoping now that it makes him forget about Merlin before that awful idea really takes hold!